Was there any way she could pull this man back from the precipice of guilt and heartbreak? "I never knew your wife, Timothy, but Ruth has told me a bit about her, and a bit more about Daniel. I don't think either one of them would want you to beat yourself up over what happened. I know you miss them. I still miss my dad, and he's been gone thirteen years."

He replied brokenly, "But my wife. My boys. I'm supposed to protect them. I failed."

She moved close enough to lay her hands on his arms. "You're not God. You couldn't have saved your family from the river any more than I could have saved my mother from tuberculosis. It's hard to go on without them, but we have to. Both of us do."

"How?" The single syllable was cut off by another sob.

"I don't know exactly. I just take one day at a time. When the hurt starts to overwhelm me, I remind myself that God understands what I can't. I don't have to explain what He allows, only trust Him to help me bear it."

He shook her hands off his arms and moved a couple of steps away. "I used to love God. How can I now? That hurts as much as anything. Now when I need Him so much, I can't feel anything toward Him except anger for what He's taken away." His voice dropped to a ragged whisper. "Sometimes I even hate Him."

JANELLE BURNHAM is from British Columbia, Canada and has been writing for over ten years. *River of Peace* is Janelle's first historical novel and is Book One of the "Stories of Peace" series from **Heartsong Presents.**

Books by Janelle Burnham

HEARTSONG PRESENTS

HP53—Midnight Music

River
of Peace

Janelle Burnham

Stories of Peace—Book One

Heartsong Presents

A note from the Author:

*To B.J. Hoff, whose stories challenge me, whose writing
inspires me, and whose friendship encourages me.*

*I love to hear from my readers! You may write to me at the
following address:*

Janelle Burnham
Author Relations
P.O. Box 719
Uhrichsville, OH 44683

ISBN 1-55748-587-9

RIVER OF PEACE

PRINTED IN THE U.S.A.

one
1930

"All off at Hythe! End of the line!"

Ida smiled at the conductor's air of importance as she stood, collecting her lunch basket and handbag. His strutting authority almost hid his inexperience, but his booming announcement to a mere handful of passengers betrayed him. Her mother would have had fun imagining how he had acquired this job and what his family was like. The thought generated a giggle, along with tears. Mom's life had been sucked away by consumption just a few months ago. Now Ida was alone at the end of the Northern Alberta Railway. A school awaited her in a town forty-five miles farther northwest, but she hadn't been told how she would get from here to there. "Looking back only keeps you from seeing opportunities," Mom had often said, along with "Ships with folded sails can't catch the wind." Despite her weariness after a full day on the train, Ida straightened her shoulders as she'd often seen Mom do when faced with uncertainty. She smoothed the folds of her heavy cape and forced herself to walk confidently toward the door.

To her surprise, a sign with her name on it swayed above the small crowd around the station. "Ida Thomas, new schoolteacher for Dawson Creek." The sign was being held by a large, brown hand, but she couldn't see the person to whom it belonged. She directed her steps toward the sign. It came down abruptly and a short, stocky person detached himself from the crowd. "Miss Thomas?"

"Yes." She extended her hand and felt it engulfed briefly

in a crushing grip.

"Lars Harper. Your trunks?" His friendly manner softened the impact of his abrupt speech.

"I have just one."

"This way." He shouldered his way through the people milling around the freight area. "Kelly." His gruff voice caught the agent's attention. "Miss Thomas' trunk and all Dawson Creek freight."

Mr. Kelly touched his hat in greeting to Ida, then gestured to the piles of boxes. "Load these into Mr. Harper's truck, Peterson."

The young assistant's gaze traveled from Ida's deep green hat down to her shoes, lingering a few moments longer than appropriate. She felt grateful for the concealing bulkiness of her cape. Having grown up in Edmonton, a new city close to the edge of the frontier, she had had to endure bold gazes such as his since her early teen years. Mom's frequent warnings about her attractive face and luxuriously thick blond hair drawing unwanted attention from uninhibited men seemed especially appropriate now. The untamed wilderness to which she'd come often attracted the same kind of men. She moved from beside Mr. Harper to slightly behind him.

"I'll take the lady's luggage." Mr. Harper addressed the agent.

"Right here." Mr. Kelly lifted the long wooden box from among the several sacks of flour. "I figured you'd be taking her with you, so I made sure Peterson put this with your freight."

"Obliged." Mr. Harper hefted the trunk without visible effort and strode purposefully toward an ancient-looking red truck. Still holding her trunk on his shoulder, he opened the passenger door and silently gestured Ida inside.

She studied her surroundings while he finished loading.

From her perspective beside the frame building, the town appeared to start with the station and extend to the east. Bright sunlight shone warmly into the truck, despite the late afternoon hour. Trees on the other side of the tracks swayed in a light wind. Blue sky and green poplar leaves provided the only colour alternative to brown dirt and buildings. A dust devil swirled toward the truck, pelting the metal with grit. The sound reminded Ida how filthy she felt. She hoped her new home wouldn't be too many hours away.

As if reading her thoughts, Mr. Harper settled himself behind the steering wheel with an abrupt announcement. "'Bout two hours to home. Horse'n wagon's a nicer trip, but truck's faster." The vehicle rumbled as he started the engine.

Having already observed that her companion wasn't a talker, Ida let her mind drift. The school committee had written to her that she would "have lodging with one of Dawson Creek's most distinguished citizens, Mrs. Barry." Using her mother's favorite way of passing time, Ida tried to picture her hostess. Probably a tall, sparse woman. "Distinguished citizen" conjured an image of more dignity than humor. She hoped she could find someone to laugh with. That's what she'd missed most since Mom died.

Mr. Harper raised his voice over the noise of the engine. "I'll answer questions if you've got 'em."

She spoke her first thought. "Do you have children in the school?"

He nodded. "Three."

"How old are they?"

"Teddy's seven, never been to school before. Nettie's ten, goin' on twenty. Thinks she knows everythin' since she can read. Jed's fifteen. Helps on the farm, so he schools part-time. Doesn't like that, but his mother's dead set on his getting an eddication."

"Is your farm near Dawson Creek?"

"Close to where the town is, but farther from where it will be." A faint smile twitched his lips.

"Pardon me?" Ida couldn't figure out how to interpret his statement.

"Thought I might stump ya." Humor in his voice removed any possible sting from his words. "Railroad guys want to build their track 'bout two miles away from where the town is. Say it's too hard to build closer, so we're movin' the town. Train won't come to us so we're goin' to it."

Silence settled once again. Ida felt uncomfortable shouting her questions, and Mr. Harper had apparently volunteered as much information as he wanted. She wouldn't have minded taking a nap, but the jolting ride made that impossible. Her driver expertly avoided the worst potholes, but the truck still bounced in and out of numerous ruts. She tried to imagine what her school would be like. The letter from the committee had said thirteen children, sometimes seventeen, so apparently three other students attended part-time like Jed Harper. She'd never taught before, as Mom had become ill shortly after Ida's graduation from Teaching School. Her trunk held many excellent textbooks, and her heart an abundance of love for children, but would that be enough? She firmly reminded herself this wasn't the time to drop anchor, as Mom would have said.

Almost two hours later, the truck labored up a steep hill. Suddenly a town sprawled before her gaze. "Is this Dawson Creek?" She tried to speak loudly enough to be heard, but without shouting.

Mr. Harper shook his head. "Pouce Coupe." The name sounded like "poos coop-ee". "Almost home, though."

Ida tried to settle the fluttering in her stomach while she took in the landscape around her. Mountains appeared distantly on the horizon. Square fields had been carved from among trees covering nearby hillsides. At least twenty shades of green blended into one another, along with the gold of wheat and ever-present dust-brown. The road curved sharply ahead of them, leading to a cluster of buildings that seemed hardly more than a hamlet.

"That's it." Mr. Harper waved his hand at the sight.

Ida hardly knew what to say. Her apprehension abated slightly as a couple of passers-by waved. The place seemed friendly enough.

"I'll take you to Mrs. Barry's right off."

Unease gripped her again. She wished irrationally that the committee had found her a hostess less distinguished. The truck stopped in front of a two-story frame house flanked by an addition on either side. Though the building appeared large in comparison to nearby houses, it would have been over-shadowed by almost any residence in Edmonton. It looked too small to house more than a small family. Mr. Harper came around to open her door, then lifted her trunk from the truck bed.

They'd taken less than a dozen steps when a short, white-haired woman hurried down the front steps. "You must be Ida Thomas, and after riding all the way from Hythe with Lars, I'm sure you're ready for a good chat. I don't suppose he thought to tell you anything!" Irrepressible twinkles in her blue eyes brought a smile to Ida's face. "I'm Lucetta Barry and delighted to have a lady with me for a change. Running a boarding house is great fun, though rather boring with only men around."

Talking continually, Mrs. Barry led Ida into a bright kitchen almost filled by an average-size table. Doors stood invitingly on either side. A third doorway across from the entrance led into a hall. Mrs. Barry gestured to the left. "Put her trunk in the yellow room, please, Lars, while I rustle up a bite to eat. You're welcome to stay, though we might be too chatty for you."

Mr. Harper's face reddened, though a grin twitched his mustache again. "Thanks, Mrs. Barry. Store's waitin'." He set the trunk by the door indicated and left with a wave for both ladies.

"I told the school committee they ought to send someone else to meet you, but Lars goes to the train every week for freight and mail so the men couldn't see why anyone else should go. Did you find out anything about us?"

Ida found herself divested of basket, handbag, and cape and gently pushed onto a chair. A steaming cup of tea flanked by a sugar bowl and a creamer appeared almost magically, followed by a dish heaped with warm rolls. "He told me his name; said he has three children—seven, ten and fifteen; the town we passed through was Pouce Coupe; and Dawson Creek is planning to move to meet the railway."

"Obviously, you've won his approval. Many people don't hear that much from him in a year. Thankfully, his Kate's more outgoing or their children may never have learned to talk."

Ida laughed delightedly. "My mother would have loved to know you. She used to make the same kinds of observations about our neighbors."

"Does she live in Edmonton?" Lively interest without a hint of nosiness sparkled in the elderly lady's eyes.

"She died this past spring from consumption." Saying the words aloud brought unexpected tears.

Mrs. Barry's face sobered compassionately, and she laid a gentle hand over Ida's fingers. "I'm sorry, dear. It's hard. I take it your father's gone, too?"

"In 1916 during the Great War." Ida smiled to let her

hostess know she didn't mind the questions.

"I lost my Kelvin at the beginning and found my William near the end, only to lose him six years later. Death always brings difficult adjustment, though the Lord's love has made it bearable for me. I hope you'll feel you can confide in me when you need a friend or even a mother."

Ida felt a bubble of joy. "I think we're already sisters in the faith."

"You look like someone who's found peace." Mrs. Barry beamed. "We can't help but be friends. Now, would you like to clean up first or unpack?"

Ida again became conscious of travel grime clinging to her. "Could I take a sponge bath?"

"I'll give you something better. I've got hot water and a big tub we can set up in your room. My son put a big stove on my back porch so I can cook and heat water in the summer without heating the entire house, the way this big cook stove does."

In less time than seemed possible, Mrs. Barry had the tub filled. "I'll put your trunk here beside your bed so you can reach clean clothes. Take as long as you like, dear." She looked closely at Ida's face. "You look exhausted and it's already past seven. Why not just tuck yourself into bed after your bath? There's a chamberpot under your bed if you need it. We can deal with unpacking tomorrow."

The suggestion sounded too good to be refused. With Lucy's help, Ida tugged her trunk inside her room. As soon as the door closed behind her hostess, she let down her hair and brushed the travel dirt from it. Short haircuts were becoming more fashionable for young ladies, but Ida had never been tempted. Her dad had loved to brush the tangles from her waist-length blond hair while she sat on his lap. Cutting her hair would feel like severing her last tie with him. With the skill of much practice, she quickly braided her smoothed hair and pinned it into a bun on the back of her head. She then lowered herself into the steaming water. What luxury! She soaked as long as she dared without falling asleep, then got out while pulling on her long-sleeved nightgown. She hadn't been in Dawson Creek a full day yet, but Mrs. Barry had already made it seem like home. Snuggling between fresh-smelling sheets, she wondered if the other residents, especially the parents of her students, would be as welcoming.

two

Ida slept deeply and peacefully. She dreamed of her mother and awoke prepared to tell her about Mrs. Barry. She opened her eyes, gazing around the pretty, well-furnished room. A nearby wall clock declared the time to be shortly after six. Already bright sunlight streamed past ruffled curtains at the windows. Mother would love the house as much as the lady who owned it. Then increasing alertness brought clear recollection. Mom was gone. That's why Ida had come here. She planned to teach, to support herself because there was no one left to do it for her.

But Mom would scold her soundly if she gave in to self-pity. "Time to set your sails," Ida reminded herself with a grin. Becoming part of this community as well as a good teacher would take hard work and determination. "But then life without challenges would be no fun," Mom had often said.

As she dressed, Ida wondered why she remembered so many of Mom's little sayings without the feelings of irritation they had brought while she was growing up. The creases had come out of her periwinkle dress nicely. Looking at the ivory lace around the stand-up collar and the French cuffs, she remembered Mom painstakingly stitching it in place. For the last several months of her life, sewing was all Mom could do without inducing the terrible coughing, so she had sewed a beautiful collection of undergarments as well as skirts, blouses, and three nice dresses. When Ida had asked where she'd found the fabric, Mom had only smiled. "I won't be leaving

13

you much money, but being well-dressed will help you make a good impression in getting a job. Besides, every time you wear these, you'll remember you're loved." Ida remembered, with tears, smiles, or sometimes both. This morning the tears came easiest. She wiped them away with the edge of the pillowcase as she made her bed.

A desk sat under her bedroom window. She seated herself for a few moments of Scripture reading. A picture-perfect view stretched before her. Sunlight brought out variations of the many shades of green she'd noticed yesterday afternoon. Dew still shimmered on the ground. Suddenly she could hardly wait for evening to see how the picture before her would change. She opened her Bible to Lamentations 3 to find the two verses which had come to mean so much to her since Mom's death. "It is of the LORD'S mercies that we are not consumed, because his compassions fail not. They are new every morning: great is thy faithfulness."* She looked out at the dew on the ground, fresh every morning like God's mercy.

Noises from the kitchen indicated Mrs. Barry had also awakened. Ida hurried out to see if she could help. Swathed in an apron covering all but the sleeves of her dress, which reached halfway between her knees and ankles, Mrs. Barry already had bacon sizzling, coffee perking, and a batch of pancake batter waiting.

"Did you leave anything for me to help with?" Ida asked in greeting.

"Good morning, dear. For this morning, no. Until you get settled in, I'd like to spoil you. But if you'd like to chat while I work, you're welcome to sit there at the table. I'll bring you a cup of tea in a jiffy, unless you'd prefer coffee." Mrs. Barry's hands didn't slow while her words tumbled out. "Chat" seemed to be one of the lady's favourite words, as well as activities.

"It's been awhile since I've had anyone to talk with this

*Lamentations 3:22, 23

early in the morning," Ida admitted. "I hadn't realized until now how much I missed it."

"Your mother?"

Ida nodded.

"What did you chat about?" Mrs. Barry set a cup of fragrant liquid in front of Ida.

"Usually what we'd read from Scripture that morning. It always seemed to get the day started right. Is this peppermint tea?"

"Made from leaves grown just outside my back door." Mrs. Barry beamed with pride. "Would you mind continuing that morning ritual with me? It's been awhile since I've been able to talk first off about God's early morning mercies."

"Actually, that's what I read this morning. The dew sparkling in the sunlight reminded me of the verses in Lamentations which talk about God's mercy being new every morning. Those thoughts have somehow kept me going almost every morning since Mom's funeral." Ida sipped the tea, hoping the hot liquid would dissolve the lump in her throat. She wanted to face her new beginning courageously, yet she still missed Mom terribly. Would she be able to become the kind of teacher Mom had wanted her to be?

Mrs. Barry let the silence linger for a few moments before replying in a gentle tone. "I know what you mean. Some verses from Isaiah did the same for me when my husbands passed away. One of these days I'll tell you about it. But for this morning, I've been thinking about Psalm 37:23 and 24. 'The steps of a good woman are ordered by the LORD: and she delighteth in his way. Though she fall, she shall not be utterly cast down: for the LORD upholdeth her with his hand.' One egg or two?"

"Just one, please." Ida laughed. "Obviously you take Scripture personally, Mrs. Barry."

She looked straight at Ida. "Is there any other way to read it?" The twinkles took over her eyes again. "You almost had me thinking you were one of those people who think the Bible is only for inspiration. And would you please call me Lucy? That's what my friends call me."

"You're so much like my mother, it won't be easy." Ida grinned. "But I'll try."

The door at the far end of the kitchen opened. "Woulda slept with them chickens if I knowed you was organizin' a Sunday mornin' gabfest," a short, wiry man growled, stumbling to the end of the table closest to him. His hair stood on end in wild disarray and his beard looked little better.

Mrs. Barry chuckled indulgently. "Miss Thomas, meet Mr. Carey, our resident grouch. Mr. Carey, meet Miss Thomas, Dawson Creek's new school teacher." She set a mug of coffee near his hand. "Mr. Carey works at the feed store, and he believes the day shouldn't start until after lunch. Three eggs or four, Mr. Carey?"

"Bein's how it's Sunday, lunch'll be pretty scarce. Better stoke up with four." He lifted his head slightly, and Ida glimpsed mischief in his eyes.

"If you'd come to church with us, you'd have plenty to eat," Mrs. Barry informed him briskly.

"Gotta write my sister a letter." Ignoring the spoon nearby, he tilted the sugar bowl so a cascade of sweetener flowed into his cup.

Lucy set a plate loaded with two pieces of toast, four pieces of bacon, and an egg in front of Ida, then looked squarely at Mr. Carey. "Is that the sister who died three years ago or the one who won't speak to you because you insulted her husband?"

Mr. Carey slurped his coffee loudly before answering. "Smart-aleck, interferin' woman! Make ya' a deal. Don't mention church for a month and I'll go with ya' once. Just once. Just to get ya' offen my back."

Mrs. Barry smiled smugly. "Deal. Now let's see if we can get you to comb your hair before you come into polite company."

Mr. Carey glared at her, then looked at Ida. "Some wimen ain't content less'n they're reformin' helpless men. How long am I gonna hafta wait for them eggs, Miz Barry?"

Lucy waved her wooden spoon at him. "S'pose I say 'until you learn to be polite.' We have a young lady with us now. Perhaps you'll brush up on your manners a bit."

"Mebbe so. Mebbe not." He muttered, taking another long slurp from his cup and reaching for the plate she extended. In an amazingly short amount of time, he inhaled four eggs, four pieces of toast, a stack of pancakes, and countless strips of bacon. "Good eats, ma'am, and welcome to Dawson Creek, Miss Thomas." The door to his room banged shut behind him.

"And so you've met your fellow boarder." Lucy sat across from Ida with a plate of pancakes and an egg. "Most of my business comes from people passing through or farm folks stranded in town by weather. I don't charge local folks anything, but they always pay me somehow, usually with food or firewood. Do you feel up to coming to church with me?"

Ida nodded. "I'm looking forward to it."

"We don't have a pastor yet, so our men take turns reading Scripture to us. Mostly we just sing and talk about God's goodness during the week. Since we don't have our own building, my son has volunteered the use of an empty one-room cabin on his farm. We hope to buy a lot at the new town site next summer and start building then. We're still a small group, so the cabin works well for now. After our meeting, we have potluck lunch. There's not much visiting time around here, so Sunday afternoons are always special."

At the little cabin, one of the men led some familiar hymns accompanied by a guitar. Another read a Scripture passage and commented on it. Prayer requests were heard and prayed over and a blessing asked over the food. Children outnumbered adults at the church service, but even the smallest sat quietly until the final "Amen" had been uttered. Ida noticed a skinny, red-haired girl leave immediately after prayer.

A woman even shorter than Ida with sparkling green eyes introduced herself right away. "I'm Nina Spencer, Lucy's daughter-in-law. My husband, Lionel, is the tallest of the men over there." Her gesture indicated a sparsely built man with a kind face and light brown hair. "I won't try to tell you which of the children in this bedlam belong to me. Maybe Mom can bring you out tomorrow for a proper visit. Come, let's fill our plates before the youngsters get all the food."

Ida ate and listened to the friendly chatter, trying to discern how these people related to each other. Four overall-clad men congregated at one end of the table and seemed to be discussing farm-related subjects. She recognized her escort from yesterday among them, though he didn't appear to be talking more than he had then.

"You must be the new schoolteacher." A well-rounded woman with blond braids wrapped around her head set a full plate on the other side of the table from Ida and continued speaking without giving Ida a chance to reply. "I'm Kate Harper. My husband met you at the train yesterday, though I don't guess he told you anything about us. We're some happy to have a proper school for our young'uns. Why'd you move all the way here from Edmonton? I know you came from Edmonton because my husband's on the school board. You don't have any family? Somehow I kind of thought you must be an orphan. You have that look about you. Well, it'll make you that much better of a teacher, I say. It's easier to relate to children when your own childhood hasn't been that happy. I hope you'll stay with us for a good long time, and that we can become friends, as long as you don't mind being friends with the parents of your students. I should actually say the mothers of your students, since it wouldn't be proper for you to be friends with their fathers. My Lars says I never give anyone else a chance to say anything, but then most people don't seem to want to talk when I'm around. If they did, they'd interrupt. Take Nina Spencer, for instance. When she wants to say something, she just starts in. That always tells me in the nicest possible way to hush up. My pa used to say I could talk the twitch right out of a cow's tail. My Lars, on the other hand, doesn't talk even when the room's silent." She laughed, an infectious, friendly sound. Before she could continue her monologue, a girl who looked almost identical to her interrupted with a heated tale of wrongdoing. Both Nina and Kate left the table temporarily to restore peace.

Ida's attention drifted to a quiet, elegantly dressed lady seated beside her. Her hair had been swept up into an attractive style contrasting sharply with the simple buns the other ladies wore, yet her shy smile betrayed no arrogance or superiority. She noticed Ida's glance and introduced herself. "I'm Cynthia Pierce. My husband's the dark-haired, handsome man sitting beside Lionel Harper."

Ida asked the logical question. "Do you have children?"

"Two with us and three with the Lord." Moisture hovered on the edges of her thickly lashed blue eyes. "My Sara is six and can hardly wait to learn to read. Theodore is 16, and a good student, too. He wants to be a doctor."

"Have you talked to him about that?" Kate had returned to her lunch. "I may be wrong, but I've never thought much—"

"Shush, Kate." Nina interrupted firmly. "We all know

learning to be a doctor is hard work, and I think it's admirable young Theo has decided to do it."

The topic of conversation changed, once again leaving Ida free to study her companions. She felt she could easily become friends with Cynthia and Nina. Kate might be more of a challenge. Her comments about Ida's past still stung, though she'd obviously had no cruel intentions. As soon as Ida learned her way around, she'd make an effort to get to know all three ladies better.

She expressed her intentions later to Lucy on the way home. "If I tried to go visiting now, I'd probably cause a town crisis by getting lost."

"You'll catch on, dear. Nina offered today to have Lionel bring her horse into town if you'd like to borrow it. She's in the family way again and won't be needing the animal over the winter."

"That would be lovely." Ida quickly recalled many visits to a horse ranch owned by a friend's father. Despite her mother's mild disapproval, Ida hadn't been able to resist the sense of freedom she felt while astride a galloping horse. "How many children do Lionel and Nina have?"

"This will be their fifth, and my seventh grandchild. My son Kelvin and his wife have two girls."

Ida thought again of the sad, young face she'd noticed during the service. "Lucy, did you notice a young girl sitting by herself near the door this morning? I didn't see her at lunch. Who is she?"

"That's young Ruth McEvan." Sadness shadowed Lucy's eyes.

"I didn't see anyone with her. What of her family?"

Lucy traced the edge of her ever-present teacup for a few moments before answering. "They came from the prairies by wagon five years ago. Last year, the mother and three children drowned in a river accident. Timothy McEvan's been a man destroyed ever since. We've offered in as many ways as we can think of to help him with the three children who are left, but he's determined to do it alone. I've never seen such a heartbroken family." She sat silently for a couple more minutes, then bustled to her feet. "Let me give you a quick tour of the house and outside before I start peeling potatoes for supper."

As Ida suspected, the door to the right near the end of the short hall led into a simple but nicely furnished parlor. "I'd like you to feel that this is your home," Lucy emphasized. "If you want to have a private conversation with any guest, feel free to bring them in here. Of course, the kitchen table is where I do most of my visiting and you're welcome to do the same." To the left, stairs led to an upper level. "This is my room." Lucy gestured toward an airy room to the left. A doorway in the center and one to the right led to two smaller bedrooms. "These rooms are perfect for overnight guests or for storing coats and sleeping children when the family comes over." They descended the stairs, and Lucy led Ida out the door at the end of the hall. To the right stood a small barn where Lucy's horse and now Ida's would be sheltered, and discreetly beyond that stood a tidy-looking outhouse. Lucy waved toward the buildings. "Lionel and his boys make sure the barn is kept clean and the horse curried. They'll take care of yours, as well. All we have to do is feed them in the morning."

"I'd like to do that," Ida offered eagerly. "Since Nina's horse will be here for my use, I'd like to help out."

"Do you have a couple of riding skirts?" Lucy glanced at the straight skirt Ida had chosen for her first Sunday.

"My mom made me a nice split skirt since she couldn't keep me from riding. She didn't think it was ladylike." Ida's cheeks warmed. She hadn't intended to sound critical of Mom.

Lucy didn't seem to notice. "Good idea. But it's probably made of heavy cotton, right?" Pausing for Ida's nod, she continued. "It will work well for now, but it won't be warm enough for winter. I have some extra wool fabric in a trunk upstairs. Would you mind if I sewed you another split skirt? You'll be spending a fair bit of time riding in the winter. We can't lose our first real teacher to frostbite." She chuckled and gave Ida a quick, one-armed hug around the shoulders.

Ida wandered to her room to finish unpacking. She already felt more loved and welcomed than she'd dared hope. Her thoughts turned back to a young face aged by grief lines and stayed with the memory until sleep took over.

three

The week passed quickly as Ida settled into her new home and acquainted herself with the town. Dawson Creek was a friendly place, with a population under fifty. As Lucy explained while drawing a map for Ida, the real centers of business in the area were Rolla, several miles to the north, and Pouce Coupe to the south, which also contained the only hospital in the area. However, each of the villages served farming families scattered throughout the Peace River region.

"When homesteaders first came west," she continued, "they built their homes as close to each other as possible. The result has been small communities of farms. You'll hear people talk about Sunset Prairie, Progress, Fellers Heights, and a host of other names. They're just clusters of farm families who've created their own community. They help each other build, plant, and harvest, as well as create schools for their children. Your school is an example."

"So the school I'll be teaching in isn't in town?"

Lucy shook her head, pushing the piece of paper across the table. "I've drawn a circle to represent Dawson Creek. These two larger circles are Rolla and Pouce Coupe. Lionel's farm is a mile due north of Dawson Creek. Lars and Kate Harper's place is also a mile north of town, but about half a mile west from Lionel's. Their land borders the farm owned by Lars' brother, James, just to the north. About a mile west of Lars' Harper is Timothy McEvan's farm, and the school is on a piece of his land closest to the road. About a mile and a half west of the school is Doug and Cynthia Pierce's place. If you ride past their farm another five miles or so and a bit to the south, you'll encounter Arras."

"That means Lionel and Nina's children are a mile and a half from school." Ida studied the map disbelievingly. "It seems like quite a distance."

"Distance is relative around here." Lucy continued her patient explanation. "We're a day's travel by horseback from the railway, so an hour's walk to school seems reasonable."

"But what about winter? I've heard it can get pretty cold in the Peace country."

"It can," Lucy said calmly. "Unless there's a good wind blowing, the children just bundle up warmly in blankets with heated rocks beside them and ride to school in the wagon. Young Lionel is good with a horse and wagon, and the other families have older sons. Except for the McEvans," she added as an afterthought. "But they're closest to the school, so walking isn't a problem. Since Nina has invited us out for a visit, how about if I take you the long way so you can get a feel for things?"

Lucy detailed her family's story while they rode. She had been born and raised in England, where she met and married her first husband, Kelvin Spencer. After his death in the early days of the War, she joined the military and met a Canadian, William Barry. After his medical discharge, they married and he brought her to the Peace area. Kelvin, Jr. chose to remain in England with his sweetheart. Lucy's younger son, Lionel, had come with his mother and step-father. "In those days," Lucy recalled, "a man could claim land just by living on it for a year and building a cabin. Lionel got his start that way, with help from the inheritance he'd received from Kelvin, Sr. Since his claim bordered William's land, when William passed away Lionel bought our farm. That money helped me set up the boarding house."

The trail branched ahead of them. Lucy slowed the horse and gestured to the left. "You can't see it from here, but the school's down that way. You'll see Lars Harper's place on the left just before we get to Lionel's."

Ida silently marveled at the rough beauty around her. She still couldn't believe young children trekked over a mile in the winter just for school. The closeness she'd observed among the families yesterday had led her to believe they lived much closer together. Instead, it appeared at least an hour's walk separated each family from another.

Lionel met them as they entered the farmyard. "Welcome, Miss Thomas. I'll take care of the horses if you ladies would like to go on inside." He helped them down from the buggy. "Nina's been hardly able to wait for you to get here."

Nina greeted each lady with a hug, then set a plate of warm cookies and cups of steaming tea on the table in front of them. "How do you like the Peace Country, Miss Thomas?"

"It's a lot different from the city, but I like what I've seen so far."

"Good. We'll do what we can to keep you here. What has Mom told you about us so far?"

"Just a basic sketch," Lucy put in. "Mostly about William and I and how Lionel got started."

Nina laughed. "The only time I've been jealous over Lionel was right after he filed the claim. There's never been anyone else for either of us since we met the first Sunday he and his mom were in Canada, but he wouldn't marry me until he had the farm going. I was only fourteen at the time. That year and a half seemed like forever." A soft smile lingered on her face as she stared out her kitchen window into the farmyard where Lionel worked with a colt in the corral. "Then one marvelous autumn day, he came calling. When I greeted him at the door, he said real solemn-like, 'Nina, I've come to speak with your father.' Dad took him out on the porch where they could be alone, but I listened at the door. 'Mr. Watson,' he said, 'I've just come from town where I deposited ten dollars from this year's crop in the bank. My farm's running well, I have all the stock and equipment I need, and I've already paid for next year's seed. I'm ready to support a wife, and I'd like to marry your daughter, with your permission, sir.' Dad didn't answer for the longest time. He and I had discussed Lionel so often, I thought I knew what he was going to say, but that pause almost had me fooled. Then he said, 'Reckon you'll have to settle that with Nina, son. But if she'll have you, my blessings on you both.' Ten years and almost six children later, here we are with twice as much land as he started with. He's a wonderful provider."

Ida met the three boys and two girls later around the lunch table. Only six-year-old Tommy had anything to say to the new schoolteacher. "I have to learn to read so I can be as smart as Young Lionel." His description of his nine-year-old brother brought smiles to all the adults' faces.

Ida commented on the children's helpfulness while she and Lucy traveled home in the buggy, with Nina's horse, Misty, plodding behind. "I've never seen youngsters so cooperative," she marveled.

"Their parents have done a great job raising them so far," Lucy agreed. "They all know nothing makes their dad more upset than for Nina to have to do something the children should have done. Even as a small boy, he used to insist on lifting pails and hauling firewood for me. He and Young Lionel come into town every evening to clean out my horses' stalls and make sure there's plenty of hay, feed, water, and firewood. In the early days of his marriage, I worried that he might be tied too tightly to my apron strings to be a good husband. Nina quickly set me straight, though. She told me one day, 'My mother always said a man will treat his wife as well or as poorly as he treats his mother. He's never neglected me to take care of you, and I'm glad to see he cares so much about your well-being.' When those two married, I definitely gained a daughter rather than losing a son."

Briefly, Ida wondered if she'd ever have a mother-in-law like Lucy, or find a husband like Lionel. But then, as Mom had often said, God brought Eve to Adam, so in the right time He'd bring the right man for Ida. "You don't have to go beating the bushes for a mate," she'd say firmly.

Ida's next discovery was the schoolhouse, built on a fenced triangle of land about six miles from town. Lucy took her there the next day, the buggy full of cleaning supplies. "It's been almost a year since the last teacher left us," she explained. "I'm sure the place is a mess."

She hadn't exaggerated. Sunlight struggled through dirt-encrusted windows. Spider webs hung from corners and desks which were covered with layers of dust. "Where were the books?" Ida asked, devoutly hoping no one had been careless enough to leave them here.

"I think the Pierces have been storing them, though we don't have a lot." Mrs. Barry opened the door of the wood stove. "Good, not many ashes. Bring me the kindling and the matches, would you, please?" In short order she had a fire blazing and a large pot of water heating.

Ida attacked the floor with a long-handled straw broom. "How many teachers have been here before?"

"Just one. He stayed for just a couple of months before the

trustees caught him coming out of the Rolla saloon. They've been searching for a replacement ever since, but no one seems to want to come this far west and north."

"Where have the children been going?"

"Most have been learning what they can at home."

"Isn't there a school in town?"

Mrs. Barry scrubbed at the bench seats with an old rag. "There is, but they've had to split it into three different locations in order to make room for all the students. A new building is planned once the town moves."

"So how did this school happen?"

"Lars, Lionel, and Timothy McEvan decided it was time they had their own school. They talked to Lars' brother James as well as Doug Pierce, and the five of them built this building on this corner of Timothy McEvan's land. That proved to be the easy part. You're the answer to our prayers about the hard part."

"Timothy McEvan. He's the man you told me about on Sunday?"

"Yes. If the school hadn't been beneficial to his children, I doubt he'd have taken any interest in the project. The way he helped us, though, showed me what a fine man hides under all that guilt and grief."

"Yoohoo. Anybody need help here?" Kate Harper peered into the room.

"You'd be welcome," Lucy responded. "I think the water's heated just perfectly, so let's start scrubbing windows. Cleaning the rest won't do any good until we can see what we're doing."

"I brought a couple of buckets and some rags." Kate bustled back to her wagon, a stream of unintelligible chatter drifting behind her. As she returned, the words began making sense.

" . . . you girls out here cleaning all by yourselves. Ruby, that's my sister-in-law," Kate offered the explanation with a glance at Ida, "is in the middle of making cheese, so she couldn't come. Nina said she'd be here later, though I'm not sure it will be good for her, and I think Cynthia's coming, too. She said something about bringing books." Kate trudged back to the wagon for more rags, so Ida took advantage of the pause.

"Will Kate's sister-in-law's family be coming to school?"

Kate overheard the question. "They will if I have to take a switch to them. James and Ruby didn't get much past the reading stage in their own schooling, so they're not too dedicated to it for their kids. That farm's all they think about. But I keep telling Ruby, it's not big enough for the whole brood. If they don't get some learning, how will they find anything else? Young Jim will try to skip as much school as he can, and his dad will let him because it means the boy can help on the farm more." She continued a commentary on each of her six nieces and nephews. ". . . and young Julie is three. Can that child ever have a fit! I'll never know how such placid parents as James and Ruby produced a temper like that one has. I love them all, but why anyone would want seven children is beyond me! Speaking of big broods, here comes Nina. Now, girls, we can't let her do anything heavy. As early in her time as she is, too much could do her harm." Kate raised her voice as Nina reached into the back of her wagon. "No, Nina, I'll carry that in for you."

Not long after Nina, Cynthia arrived with several crates of books. She rolled up the sleeves of her fashionable print dress and started scrubbing book shelves. By the middle of the afternoon, the schoolhouse gleamed. Sunlight streamed through clean windows onto well-dusted desks. Just inside the door, a clean washbasin sat on a wooden table.

"What are those pegs for?" Ida asked, looking at the double row just above the washstand.

"Towels," Kate informed her. "Each child will bring his or her own towel and cup. The men will keep the water bucket filled before winter. Once the snow starts, you can melt it for washing and drinking water. You won't believe how dirty the children can get just during a brief recess. Mark my words, you'll be glad for those towels before the first day is out."

Despite her interaction with her students' mothers, Ida still felt unprepared. She had no doubts about her academic abilities. But could she meet the needs of seventeen students? Thirteen to seventeen distinct personalities? She wished Mom were here, too, with some helpful advice.

She walked to school the first day to get a feeling for the trek her students would make every day. Teddy and Nettie Harper arrived only a few minutes after she'd settled at her desk. Nettie not only resembled her mother in appearance, but also in behavior. Her "Good morning, Miss Thomas," was quickly followed by, "Teddy's shy, but I'm not. My cousin, Patricia, taught me to read after her mother taught her. I've read every book Mrs. Spencer's loaned me, plus Mama's Bible twice. I can help you teach the little kids if you want."

Ida welcomed them both with a smile, recognizing thirst for learning behind Nettie's self-importance. She greeted other new arrivals, grateful for a reason not to answer Nettie's offer. After a brief Scripture reading and a quick prayer, she began sorting the children into groups. Five youngsters were eager to learn to read—Tommy Spencer and Teddy Harper, as well as red-haired, freckle-faced Phillip McEvan whose brown eyes invited mischief, shy Karin Harper, and dainty Sara Pierce. Ida assigned Teddy a seat as far from Nettie as she could manage, sensing the boy needed a break from his overbearing older sister. On the other hand, their cousin Karin looked like she might burst into tears any time she lost sight of Patricia, one of Ida's oldest students. Karin had to be on the front row with the rest of the new readers, so Ida asked Patricia to sit right behind her. Little Sara Pierce kept looking around for her older brother, but seemed content as long as she could see Theodore.

The rest of the students sorted themselves out as Ida asked questions about their knowledge and abilities. Patricia's assigned seat to the left of the classroom caused the older students to gather there, as well. The part-time students had come for the first day, so they staked out their seats at the back. Justin Harper's eyes sparkled as Ida asked him arithmetic questions of increasing difficulty. When he finally paused over an algebra problem, she guessed he'd probably be ready for graduation by the end of the year, along with Theodore Pierce. Jed Harper was somewhat behind Justin and Theodore in academic ability and not quite as eager to learn. His cousin, Jim, obviously didn't want to be in school, though he treated Ida with courtesy. During harvest, Patricia Spencer and Ruth McEvan would be Ida's only students in the older group.

Ruth McEvan remained a mystery. She rarely spoke, even when spoken to. Ida handed her one of the newest readers available. The girl's eyes sparkled briefly, then resumed their sad, almost hardened gaze. She answered Ida's questions so quietly the teacher had to strain to hear her. Ida also noticed that Theodore waited until Ruth had chosen a seat, then picked one beside her for himself.

Aside from Ruth, Ida felt her biggest challenges would be among the middle group. David Spencer seemed quiet for an eight-year-old, reluctant to interact with others. His older brother, Young Lionel, seemed a typical nine-year-old boy, despite his air of responsibility. Ida could tell he'd been told to watch out for the younger ones. Michael Harper was obviously a typical ten-year-old, full of energetic ideas for getting reactions out of others, particularly Nettie, whom he teased to distraction. His younger sister, June, obviously would have preferred to be outside climbing trees. With the others' distinct and attention-grabbing personalities, Clara Spencer's quiet studiousness could be easy to overlook.

After getting her students seated and organized, Ida assigned all but the youngest a short exercise in which they were to write one page about themselves. She gave the five youngest students a bucket of colored blocks which she asked them to organize according to colour and size. Though both assignments would help her understand her students better, they also gave Ida a few moments to collect her thoughts and watch the students as a whole.

It wouldn't be difficult to distinguish among the family groups, she decided. All of James and Ruby Harper's children looked typically Scandinavian—stocky build, white-blond hair, and blue eyes. Both McEvan children had red hair and freckled noses. Theodore and Sara Pierce were black-haired, though Sara's eyes were blue while Theo's were dark brown. Jed Harper was the image of his dad, and his sister and brother looked too much like their mother to be mistaken for their cousins. The four Spencers varied most in appearance, but Ida felt better acquainted with them than the rest of her students. She hoped that feeling wouldn't last long.

By two o'clock, Ida felt grateful she had arranged for classes to let out early. Many of the children were over-excited, making discipline difficult to maintain. The younger ones had become fidgety, and the older ones were obviously ready to escape their studies. An hour later, after they had departed, she closed the door with a sigh.

"Surely teaching school isn't that bad already," a male voice interrupted her thoughts.

She turned her head with a start in the direction of the voice to find a well-dressed young man lounging against a tree. He looked vaguely familiar and his smile seemed pleasant enough, so she smiled back. "The first day is always tough."

"Then it's good I'm here to carry your books home for you. I'm Ken Danielson. I didn't get an opportunity to introduce myself at church a week ago." He reached out a hand for the textbooks from which she planned to create special assignments for Justin and Theo.

She let him take the books, while declining to place her hand on the arm he offered. "I'm afraid I've met so many people these last two weeks, I don't remember seeing you. But thanks for the escort, just the same."

"I'll bring the buggy tomorrow."

His assumption that his presence would be welcome annoyed her. "That won't be necessary. I'll be on horseback. Besides, I enjoy the time by myself after the children go home."

"We can tie your horse behind. I want to get well acquainted with you." He winked flirtatiously.

Ida decided not to press the point for the time being. They discussed general topics—weather, town news, and harvest, though he didn't seem to know much about the latter. At the end of the boardwalk leading to her new home, she stopped and reached for her books. "Thanks for escorting me home, Mr. Danielson. I'll see you Sunday?"

A glimmer of something uncertain showed in his eyes before it was quickly replaced with a smooth smile. "Or perhaps before, Miss Thomas." He lifted his hat in salute and left her wondering who on earth he really was.

four

The next month passed more quickly than Ida would have believed possible. Though her classroom had appeared to organize itself into three groups on the first day, by the end of the first week, she felt as if she were teaching thirteen different classes. Even her new readers were at different levels. Sara Pierce already knew her letters, while Teddy Harper still struggled distinguishing colors. Tommy Spencer learned his letters quickly, as long as Young Lionel was at school. The days his older brother stayed home, Tommy's mind seemed everywhere but on his studies. Karin Harper soaked up schooling like a thirsty sponge and would catch up to Sara in no time. Hopefully the two girls would help each other once they learned to read. Then there was Phillip McEvan—mischievous, energetic, affectionate Phillip. He liked nothing better than to sit on his teacher's lap and would have spent every recess there if Ida would have let him. He greeted her each morning with a hug, began and ended each recess with a hug, and wouldn't leave in the afternoon without a hug.

"The child seems starved for affection," Ida explained to Lucy one evening during the second week. "I don't want to appear to play favorites, but denying him a hug or a cuddle seems as bad as slapping one of the other children."

"How does Ruth treat him?" Lucy's hands stilled in their work for once as she gave complete attention to Ida's answer.

Ida couldn't help the sigh that felt like it came from her toes. "She's another challenge. I've tried several times to get her to talk with me, but all I get are one-word answers.

She seems as close to happy as she ever gets when left completely alone. Her sadness is like a shield against life in general, including her little brother."

"Does he try to hug her?"

"Usually he just tries to hold her hand. She'll tolerate him for a few minutes, then makes him let go."

"Does she have any friends?"

Ida grinned. "Theodore Pierce. She tries to ignore him like she does the rest of us, but he never gives up. He brings treats for her lunch and often walks her to and from school."

Lucy resumed stirring her cake batter. "Sort of like another young man I often see at the end of my boardwalk."

"If I felt he were as much my friend as Theo is Ruth's, I wouldn't work so hard at avoiding him." She felt surprised at how easy it was to talk to Lucy, almost like old times with Mom.

"Why do you say that, dear?" Lucy poured the batter into two round pans which she placed in the oven. She dipped steaming water out of the boiler on the back of the stove into the dishpan. Ida would have liked to help her, but Lucy preferred to let the dishes air dry. She used rinse water so hot the dishes were ready to put away by the time she finished wiping the counters.

"He talks mostly about himself and his own world. He's nice enough, but he doesn't seem interested in me as a person. He tries too hard to impress me."

Lucy poured a cup of tea for each of them and settled at the end of the table where Ida had been grading arithmetic quizzes. "Oh?"

"Oh, yes. I know all about how his dad was one of the town's earliest businessmen and now owns the only hardware store. As a result, his family is so well off, Ken doesn't have to work, which is why he can meet me after school almost every day. Then you should hear him talk about his concern for Dawson Creek's spiritual well-being. Apparently the entire community is comprised of unrepentant reprobates." Ida couldn't stop her giggle.

Lucy grinned in response. "Has he mentioned the Presbyterian group who meet at James and Ruby's place twice a month, or the Catholic priest who comes through on a regular basis? There's also an Anglican church being planned for building in Rolla next summer."

"Like I say, if he didn't try so hard, I might be more impressed."

"And how's Nettie doing?" Lucy's eyes twinkled, remembering the girl's eagerness to be in charge.

"Periodically I have to remind her who the teacher is and who is really responsible for keeping discipline in the classroom. Mostly, I just try to keep her so busy she doesn't have time for meddling."

"Is that difficult?"

"Yes and no. She has learned quite a bit on her own, but only what she wanted to learn. She can whip right through the eighth level readers, but anything more than simple arithmetic is difficult. It's easy to find plenty she needs to work on. Motivating her to do it is the hard part."

"You're showing a lot of wisdom in working with those youngsters, Ida. Your mother would be proud of you." Lucy patted Ida's arm. "God sent you here for a special reason. I'm more convinced of that by the day. And also grateful He put you with me."

Unexpected tears filled Ida's eyes. Lucy had an uncanny knack for finding her sore spots and saying just the right thing to ease them. "Thanks, Lucy. Some days I wonder if I really am fulfilling a purpose or just muddling through."

Lucy's voice softened. "I can imagine. But isn't that what

the New Testament calls walking by faith? It seems to us we're just muddling through. But our Father sees the whole picture and orders our steps accordingly."

"I know He ordered my steps to put me here," Ida replied, putting her hand over Lucy's. "I don't know how I would have managed these first few months without Mom if I hadn't been with you. Still, though, I would want her to be proud of what I'm doing if she were here. But if she weren't gone, I wouldn't be here." She laughed self-consciously. "Don't I sound mixed up?"

Lucy blinked away tears of her own. "It is hard getting used to being without those we love. I hope you won't be reluctant to let me know when you need some mothering."

"A hug right now would be nice." *Would that assuage the torrent of insecurity a difficult school day seemed to bring?*

Without hesitation, Lucy enfolded Ida in a loving hug. She said nothing else, just simply held the younger woman tightly until Ida relaxed her own embrace to reach for her handkerchief.

"Thanks. I'd hoped I'd miss her less with being busy, but it seems I miss her more."

"That's the way it is, honey, at least for the first little while. As long as you don't try to avoid the pain, it will get easier in time."

Ida stacked her papers. "I'm going to go to bed early. By the way, I won't be here for supper tomorrow evening. The Pierces have invited me out to their farm. I'll walk to school in the morning, and Mr. Pierce will drive me in after supper."

"That's lovely." Lucy's face beamed. "I knew it wouldn't take folks long to want to get acquainted. Are you having any trouble with the schoolhouse stove? It can be difficult at times."

Ida wrinkled her forehead in puzzlement. "I haven't had to

do much with it. Since it's started getting cold overnight, I've found a fire already built when I arrive each morning. The boys keep it stoked during the day, and all I have to do is close the dampers before I leave in the afternoon."

"You have no idea who's doing it?"

"No. The schoolhouse is nice and warm when I get there, so whoever it is comes fairly early."

"That's quite a trek for anyone. Probably if you're supposed to know who it is, you'll find out eventually." Lucy shrugged and grinned.

Except for her mysterious morning visitor, "getting acquainted" hadn't been a problem for Ida. Not only did she see most of her students and their families on Sundays, but one parent or another usually stopped by the schoolhouse every day. Nina had invited Ida and Lucy for a meal at least once a week since school started. Friendship grew quickly between the two younger women. Kate Harper visited regularly, almost always on Saturdays, and she'd already had Ida out to their farm for a supper. With Nina's assistance, Ida was learning to understand Kate and even appreciate the caring she concealed behind unending talk. Timothy McEvan remained the only parent whom Ida hadn't met.

Having seen Spencers' log farmhouse and Lars Harpers' log cabin, Ida was awed by the gracious frame home in which the Pierces lived. Surrounded by a whitewashed picket fence, the house looked like it had been transplanted from one of the city's nicest neighborhoods. "What a lovely house!" she couldn't resist exclaiming as she, Theodore, and Sara walked up the drive.

"Father always says this is Mother's reward for being willing to live out at the edge of nowhere so he can have the farm he wants." Theo's ready smile lit his eyes.

"I'll show you my room," Sara offered, eager to have some

of Teacher's attention, too.

Actually, Ida received a grand tour of the entire home, conducted by both her students. Theo's explanations gave her a sense of the life from which his mother must have come, while Sara's comments told her what a loving atmosphere Cynthia had created for her family. When they finished, Cynthia had tea and dainty cookies waiting in the sitting room.

"Doug won't be in from the field until dark, around seven," she explained, "so I thought a little refreshment would keep us going until supper time. Have you washed?" She examined Sara's hands gently. "Go wash your hands and face and comb your hair. We won't eat everything before you get back." She hugged the small girl and gave her a kindly push toward the small room beside the porch. Ida had never before seen a room set aside exclusively for washing and bathing.

Theo had obviously anticipated his mother's expectations. His hair looked damp from where he'd used water to help tidy it. Though the tea cup and saucer looked too dainty for his hands, which were beginning to look like a man's, he handled them expertly. He responded to his mother with surprising gentleness and deference, though without appearing like an over-mothered sissy. After about thirty minutes, he excused himself for chores.

"So how do you like teaching school?" Cynthia inquired. Though her voice carried unmistakable traces of her cultured background, it communicated genuine interest.

"It's a challenge." Ida smiled reassuringly at Sara. "I have five new readers, each of whom is at a different level. It's sort of that way throughout the entire classroom."

"I've spent some time working with Sara here at home. Would there be anything I could do to help?" Cynthia's eyes lit eagerly. "I've already asked Doug, and he wants me to do whatever I can."

"From what I've seen of Sara's learning, I think you could help me quite a lot. Most of my work with her age group is just repetition. How about if you come in whenever you're able, and I promise I'll be able to put you to work."

"I would really enjoy that. I've always loved children and wanted a houseful of my own. Somehow, though, I've only been able to keep two." She scooped Sara close to her with a fierce hug. "And I love them both dearly."

She declined Ida's offer of help with the tea tray or with supper. "You've had a long day. I'd be pleased if you could just relax while I finish in the kitchen. If you'd like, help yourself to one of our books, or if you prefer to nap, Sara can show you to the guest room."

Ida smiled her thanks. "A book sounds wonderful. I've had little time to read just for enjoyment since school started."

Theo's attitude toward his mother explained itself as soon as Doug Pierce entered the house. Ida noticed he stopped first at the washroom to clean off the dirt of the field. He then vanished upstairs to return quickly, clad in clean pants and a fresh shirt. His light brown hair had been dampened and combed into place. Only then did he venture toward the kitchen, where Ida could hear him greet his wife. When Cynthia called everyone to the table a short time later, Doug helped her carry serving dishes from the kitchen, then held her chair for her as she sat down. He and his son then seated themselves. After asking the blessing, he made sure his wife was served first.

The adults' conversation soon expanded to include Theo and Sara. Ida was impressed with the way both parents gave importance to their children's opinions and thoughts.

"When is the town going to move?" Theo asked his dad, following Ida's account of her trip from Hythe with Lars Harper.

Doug stacked dishes while his wife brought out bowls of fluffy vanilla pudding topped with fresh raspberries and whipped cream. "Last I heard, it's scheduled for mid-November."

"How do you move a town?" Sara wanted to know.

"Mr. Harper told me they'll use huge chains to hook a building to a big machine or maybe to horses which will tow it," Theo explained patiently.

The tiny girl looked puzzled. "What's tow?"

Her dad laughed. "That means to pull. The buildings will roll on logs which will be on top of planks."

Sara's brow remained wrinkled. "I still don't understand."

"That's okay," her mother reassured. "It's hard to explain. We'll have to take you to watch."

"But what if I'm in school?"

Doug tweaked her braid. "We'll work out something, sweetheart."

Ida already knew what would be worked out. Listening to the family talk, she'd decided to cancel classes so families could watch the event together. The process sounded mysterious even to her. It promised to be an exciting event that would draw spectators from miles around.

Theo offered to drive her home. Ida was delighted his father agreed. Theo probably had some insight she needed, but she didn't think he'd want to discuss it with a group, even if that group were simply his parents. Besides, darkness made it easier to share confidences.

She hugged Sara goodbye, thanked Cynthia for the delightful meal, and shook Doug's hand. Theo helped her into the buggy. She waited until they were out of the yard before she asked, "May I ask you some personal questions, Theo?"

His voice in the dark sounded perplexed. "Sure, Miss Thomas."

"I've noticed your efforts to befriend Ruth McEvan. How well do you know her?"

He didn't answer right away. "Probably as well as anyone, though you've probably noticed she doesn't give much more attention to me than to others. Why?"

"I'm worried about her."

"Me too." His voice sounded heavy with the weight of his concern.

"Has she told you what's troubling her?"

"Do you know what happened to her mother and brothers?"

"Yes."

"We've talked about it some after church or on the way home from school. She thinks it's her fault, and that she has to make it up to her dad and other two brothers."

"There's another brother?"

"Greg. He's only three, a lot like Phillip, but quieter."

"Does anyone help them, like cooking, cleaning, sewing, that kind of thing?"

"Mr. McEvan and Ruth won't let them. They both insist they can do everything themselves."

Ida couldn't imagine the fourteen-year-old girl being mother and housekeeper as well as going to school. No wonder she kept to herself. She didn't have time for normal, childhood friendships—except for this friend who wouldn't let her be alone. "How does she find time for her studies?"

"She's real smart, Miss Thomas. Most of her work she can do in school. If she does have to study at night, her dad makes supper and takes care of the boys." His tone told how proud he felt of her accomplishment.

"Do you mind if I ask why you work so hard to be her friend? It seems to me if it weren't for you, she'd let herself be alone."

He paused again. "That's why I do it. She doesn't know yet how much a friend can help. So I stick close for when she realizes she needs someone."

"That shows a lot of caring and maturity on your part, Theodore. More than most fellows your age." She wasn't sure how he'd respond to the praise, but she had to tell him how she felt.

"My dad's the same way—always helping the folks that don't think they need it. He says that's what Jesus did for us, dying for us before we realized we were sinners. He says a true friend is the kind that doesn't expect anything in return. People respect my dad. Some of the ones he helped are the ones who were there for us when Mother got so sick. He also says true friends are there when no one else wants to be. Ruth tries to make people not want to be around her, so I just stick that much closer. She'll be all right one of these days."

Ida felt like she'd lost her breath. With heart and understanding such as his, this boy—no, young man—would make a fantastic doctor. "What if Ruth never changes, Theo?"

"She will. God told me so."

His quiet confidence shook Ida afresh. "Would you mind telling me how you know for sure?"

"I was praying for her one morning while reading my Bible, and I saw a verse I'd never seen before. It says, 'Weeping may endure for a night, but joy cometh in the morning.'* I know God never lies."

They had reached the edge of town, so Ida spoke quickly. "Sorry for all the questions, Theo, but I have one more. You've told me some pretty personal things tonight. Why did you trust me so easily?"

He didn't answer until he stopped the horses in front of Ida's boardwalk. "Partly because I know you really care about all of us, that you're our friend."

*Psalms 30:5

Ida didn't want to pry, but she sensed the unspoken part of his answer was the most important. "Can you tell me the other part?"

"You won't tell anyone else?"

"No. Everything you've said tonight stays with me."

"The first Sunday I saw you, I felt like God told me you are the person He'll use to help Ruth."

five

When Ida looked out her window Wednesday morning, she gasped with surprise. A thick white layer of snow coated everything. She dressed quickly and hurried out to the kitchen. "Lucy, did you notice what happened last night?"

"That there's snow," Mr. Carey responded from where he sat at the kitchen table still slurping coffee. "It's part of the scenery most of the year hereabouts."

"She knows that, you old grouch," Lucy fussed, filling a plate for Ida. "It is pretty, isn't it?"

"Misty won't have any trouble in it, will she?"

"It might take her a few minutes to adjust, but she'll do fine." Lucy patted Ida's shoulder reassuringly. "At least the school will be warm when you get there." Her eyes twinkled over the mystery.

"I suspect Theo comes over early, since they live nearby." Ida returned to her room for warmer clothing. She tugged on the beautiful woolen riding skirt Lucy had made, then folded another skirt into her bag. A shelter for the horse had mysteriously appeared near the school about a week after school started. With its door closed, she had a private place to change into more appropriate clothing for the day.

"Theo's sure a fine young man, isn't he?" Lucy called through the closed door.

Ida fastened her heavy black woolen cape around her neck. This was the first time she'd worn this garment since Mother had finished it the week before her death. She swallowed back the inevitable tears before answering. "He is." She came back into the kitchen, tying a pink knitted scarf around her head. "He hasn't missed a day of school yet. Even when the other boys are helping with harvest and butchering, he's at school. I wonder how Doug manages without him."

"I wouldn't know, but from what Doug and Cynthia were saying during lunch on Sunday, they're just as eager for him to become a doctor as he is. Maybe Doug's making a few sacrifices of his own to make sure his boy gets a good education."

"I'm glad, and a little scared if they consider my teaching good education." Ida laughed, trying not to remember Mother's pale face as she'd sewn the big pink buttons down the front of this cape and the pink trim around the edges.

"From watching the pains you take here at home and the way you worry over those children, I haven't a doubt they're getting the best education possible." Lucy gave Ida a floury hug. "Oops, didn't mean to get breadmaking all over your lovely cape." Her voice softened. "Is that another of your mother's projects?"

She nodded.

"Wear it like a hug, girl. Let it remind you of her love, not just her absence."

Ida squeezed her friend's sticky hands. "Thanks, Lucy. Now I've got to get out of here. The children will never let me live it down if I arrive after they do."

"My prayers are with you!" Lucy called out the back door.

Ida saddled Misty almost without thinking about it. Riding had grown from an enjoyable recreation to an instinctive part of her life in the past weeks. She breathed deeply of the crisp, clean air, wondering briefly if this kind of life would have restored Mother's health. Then the rhythmic clop of Misty's hoofs and the stillness of winter's first morning replaced her sadness with peace. Lucy had been right. Time made grief easier to carry—not less, just easier.

What would it take to help Ruth and her dad discover that secret? Ida had tried everything she knew to find a crack in Ruth's self-imposed barrier. She'd even borrowed Lucy's buggy for one day so she could offer Ruth and Phillip a ride home.

"Thanks, Miss Thomas, but we wouldn't want to trouble you. It's not that far, anyway." Ruth had grasped her brother's hand and they had set out before Ida could think of a reply.

Ida remembered Theo's gentle defense. "She doesn't mean to be rude, ma'am. I think she actually likes you."

Ida had turned to her young friend in amazement. "Where did you get that idea?"

He'd smiled. "I've seen her watching you. She adds bows and lace bits to her blouses like you do, and even tries to walk like you."

Now, as she rode Misty through the new snow, she wondered again if his conviction about her helping Ruth wasn't the product of his caring imagination. Yet Lucy's comment about Ida's special purpose in Dawson Creek added validity to Theodore's idea. *Or was it God's idea?*

To Ida's surprise, a new face appeared at the dinner table that evening. Lucy introduced the light-haired man as Pete Miller. "He's a carpenter from Grande Prairie come to help with the move. He'll be here a month or so."

"Where is Grande Prairie?" Ida wondered.

Their guest didn't seem bothered by her ignorance. "It's a ways south of Hythe."

"How will you be helping?"

"Some of the old buildings need reinforcement, and there's a heap of new ones being built at the new site. You'll find yourselves overrun with carpenters in the next few days. Seems to be plenty to keep us all busy. Sure is good food, ma'am," he complimented Lucy.

Maybe Pete could explain something Ida had noticed yesterday. "Can you explain the shallow holes being dug behind some of the buildings?"

"I'd be glad to. They're to make room for skids."

"What are skids?"

He took a couple swigs of coffee before answering. "It's what they call the lumber they put under the building to make it easier to move. If the building wasn't on the skids, it would be pulled apart when they drag it to the new site."

A few days later, Ida saw a different approach to the same task. It took her a few moments to realize what looked different about the boarding house. Gradually she realized boards around its base had been removed, revealing the stone pilings on which it sat. According to Pete, there was just enough distance for skids between the base of the house and the ground. One by one, homes and businesses began disappearing from the old town site. Some were slowly dragged by the large crawler tractors that had been used to construct the railroad grade. Others were pulled by farm tractors, and horses moved the rest.

Lucy and Ida visited the new town site Saturday afternoon. Several houses and stores had already been settled on new foundations, while brand new buildings stood in various stages of construction nearby. Pete had been right about the number of carpenters who had come to participate in the building boom. Most of them chose to stay at the three-story Dawson Hotel, which took the better part of two weeks to relocate. As it crawled along towed by horses, guests wandered in and out just like it was stationary.

The boardinghouse moved on Tuesday. Ida and Lucy packed all their breakables into crates padded with linens and removed wall hangings. Lucy used the crates to brace cupboard doors closed.

"Think you can find your way back this afternoon? Home will be two and a half miles farther away." Lucy giggled at her own joke.

The old town site looked strange when Ida rode by after school. Now that the boardinghouse was gone, she also noticed how many other buildings had been moved. Another home was being prepared while she watched.

The school trustees had given Ida permission to cancel school the next day so everyone could watch the Co-op store being moved. She and Lucy spent the early part of the day putting their belongings back in order. Mr. Carey came in for lunch, mumbling the entire time.

"Who's lousy idea was this anyway? Buildings weren't made to be moved like someone's satchel. It's easier to lay railroad track than it is an entire town. And people are acting like it's some big party, all lined up out there waiting for the Co-op like it's the Queen or something."

Lucy had prepared ham and beans, and she set a steaming plate in front of him. "I'm sure a warm, healthy lunch will help you feel better."

"And what if I don't want to feel better! That's the trouble with this world. Wimen always tryin' to fix things!" He wolfed his lunch in six bites and stomped back out the door.

"Poor man. It's so hard to stay grouchy when this world is full of excitement." Lucy giggled, dipping herself another small helping of beans. "More for you, dear?"

"No thanks. I've had plenty. It was delicious as usual."

Lucy grinned again. "When you've had as much practice as I've had, you'd better know how to make a meal tasty."

By the time they finished dishes, the Co-op was within sight. They grabbed thick coats, shoved their feet into warm boots, and rushed outside to join the crowd across from the store's new location. The store's skids rested on logs that rolled across planks laid along the ground. Ropes connected the building to the bottom of a large metal post, which had been secured in a hole some distance away. A horse had been hitched to each of four poles extending at right angles from the post. As they circled the post repeatedly, the ropes wound around the post, towing the building so slowly it barely seemed to move. A crew of men formed a continuous chain of activity, picking up planks and logs from behind the building and repositioning them in front. Meanwhile, a stream of people wandered in and out of the store.

"They said they wouldn't close for a moment during the move. I think most people are just going in to see what it's like in a moving building." Kate Harper's familiar voice nearby caught Ida's attention.

She looked over at her friend. "And have you been shopping today?"

Kate's face turned faintly pink, and she nodded. "Of course. We were almost out of flour."

"Miss Thomas!"

Ida felt a small body hurl itself at her knees as her legs were caught in a vice-like grip. She looked down at disheveled red hair. "Phillip! I'm glad to see you." She pried his arms away from her legs so she could bend down and return his hug. "What are you doing today?"

"Ruth and Papa wanted to see the store, and I wanted to see you. Will you come with me? I want to show you my little brother." Phillip hopped from one leg to another in his excitement.

She let the small boy grab her hand and drag her down the block. "Papa! Papa! I found Miss Thomas." Ruth stood beside a tall, red-haired man who looked like he hadn't eaten a decent meal in months. His clothes hung on him as though he had once been stockier. *He would have been a huge man*, Ida thought, imagining him big enough to fit his coat properly.

A smile stretched the man's mouth, but didn't touch his grief-filled blue eyes. "Was she lost?"

"No. But she's my teacher and I wanted Greggy to see her." Phillip tugged at the foot of a small red-haired boy his father held. Mr. McEvan placed the boy on the boardwalk so the youngsters could talk. Ida knelt down to be at the boys' eye level. "Greggy, this is Miss Thomas. She's the pretty lady I told you about. She's teaching me to read so I can teach you. She likes hugs, too." Phillip demonstrated his point by giving his teacher another neck-crushing embrace. Before she could return it, Greg had joined the hug.

Ida squeezed them both, then kept her arms around them while she chatted. "How old are you, Greg?"

"Free." He struggled to show her on the fingers of one hand while putting his other thumb in his mouth.

"Do you help your Papa at home while Phillip goes to school?"

The boy nodded solemnly.

"I'm teaching him his letters like you teach me," Phillip informed her. "He wants to come to school when he's as big as me."

"I'm sure he'll be as good a student as you are." Ida hugged them both again before standing up. She lifted her gaze to find their dad watching her. "I'm pleased to have met you, Mr. McEvan."

"Likewise," he replied gruffly with a stiff nod. "You've been good to my children."

She didn't know how to reply. The pain in his eyes grabbed her heart. She had a crazy impulse to embrace him as she had his sons, as if by doing so she could absorb some of his agony. She met Ruth's gaze, surprised to see a hint of friendliness there. "I'm glad to see you, too, Ruth." Without thinking, she hugged the girl. To her amazement, she felt the hug returned.

Greg and Phillip were now busy drawing designs in the mud made by melting snow, chatting happily to each other. Ida didn't know what to say in parting. Neither Ruth nor her father offered any comment.

"Miss Thomas!" Ken's friendly greeting interrupted the almost-awkward silence. He strode quickly toward them. "The cafe windows face this way. Please share a soda with me while we watch."

His almost childish enthusiasm grated on her nerves. But maybe his carefree approach was what she needed to break the spell McEvans' sadness had put over her. She patted Ruth's shoulder as she smiled at Ken. "Sure. See you tomorrow, Ruth."

Ken extended his elbow but Ida declined the offer. "How did your parents' store survive the move?"

"No problems at all. We thought about leaving the house at the old site and building new here, but Father didn't think we could be finished before winter."

She noted his inference that weather, not money, had been the deciding factor. At least she needn't feel guilty about him spending money on her, she mused while waiting for him to return to the table with their treat. Spending money seemed to be his favorite form of entertainment.

The massive soda glass he carried almost overflowed as he set it down. "Doesn't that look tasty. Here, I brought an extra spoon."

She couldn't remember having ever tasted anything so rich. "Mmmm. It's almost addicting." She smiled her thanks before taking another bite.

"I've been thinking about this new house of my parents'," he commented several mouthfuls later. "Spring might be a good time for me to build a house of my own so they wouldn't have to build with me in mind. What do you think?"

Ida almost choked on her ice cream. What did it matter what she thought? "It could be a practical idea, if that's what you really want to do. Do you know for sure you're going to settle in Dawson Creek?"

"If I decide to move, I can just sell the house. But I probably won't be leaving for awhile."

Ida wondered if he'd finally found employment that interested him, but was afraid to ask. Ken's continuing monologue relieved her of the need to reply.

"I've always wanted to travel a bit, but I'm not wild about doing it alone. I just realized I could get the house started in the spring, leave on a honeymoon right after school's out, and the house would be finished by the time we got back."

She choked back laughter. "How long would this honeymoon be?"

"Six months at least. Oh look, they've just about got the store in place! Isn't it just amazing the way we've been able to relocate this entire town?" His tone made it sound as though he'd played a vital role in the move.

"Mrs. Barry's probably looking for me. Thanks for the soda."

Ken stood with her. "I'll escort you back. No telling what could attack you in this wild town."

Ida looked at him with a smile, expecting to see an answering twinkle over the joke. Instead, she could tell he took himself quite seriously. The notion strengthened her impulse to giggle. She held the laughter back, not wanting to hurt his feelings.

Both she and Lucy did laugh out loud later when she

related the story. "That boy has no more sense of reality than Nina's new baby, Tabitha." Lucy shook her head.

"Besides, if I were in any danger, I'd want a man with working muscles, not a storekeeper!" Ida giggled again. Then a stray thought doused her mirth. Timothy McEvan had obviously been quite solidly built at one time. Could misplaced guilt over being unable to protect his family be what troubled him? As though a cloud had passed over the sun, she no longer felt like laughing. Somehow the McEvans' grief had made its way into her heart.

six

School demanded all Ida's patience Thursday. A day off had left the children as fidgety and excitable as they usually were on Mondays, except she didn't have Cynthia's help as she did at the beginning of the week. Anticipating some of the excitement, she had planned some discussion for the beginning of the day. Each child had an opportunity to tell what he or she had seen or heard. They would have dragged the conversation out all day if Ida would have let them. She set the youngest students to drawing pictures of the move and asked Ruth, Patricia, and Theodore to write essays about it. The three older boys were missing this week to help with the butchering.

"Time for arithmetic drills," she announced to the middle group. "I've written addition problems on the board. As soon as I say 'Go', you write down answers as quickly as you can. Ready, set, go!"

Usually the informal competition motivated each of the children to work as hard as they could. Today, Nettie deliberately set her pencil down in the middle of the paper and stared out the window. It seemed like an attention-getting scheme, so Ida ignored her. A squabble broke out among the younger students. While she tried to settle the disagreement, she heard an irritated exclamation from David.

"Nettie! I'm trying to work."

"You're as boring as Teacher," Nettie whispered back.

Ida stood as quickly as she could without tripping on her skirt. "Nettie Harper, sit down."

Nettie deliberately walked away from her desk. The altercation had gripped everyone's attention by this time. Even the older students had ceased writing. Ida knew she had to handle Nettie carefully or lose any discipline she'd carefully cultivated so far.

"Nettie, if you take another step, you can keep walking until you get home." She kept her voice calm.

"Makes me no never mind." Nettie tossed her head. "You don't like me anyway."

Ida fervently wished Nettie would have chosen a more private moment for her declaration. As it was, the challenge had to be answered before the entire school. She wondered if Jed's absence had anything to do with Nettie's timing. "How about if you come sit down, and we'll all talk about it?"

"You can't make me."

You need a good spanking, Ida thought, even while acknowledging that solution would only embarrass and alienate Nettie. Somehow, though, she had to overcome the child's will. "Nettie, you can either discuss this with all of us now, or I personally will take you home and explain to your dad what has happened." If she had to, she'd leave Theo in charge.

After an interminable pause, Nettie's defiant gaze dropped, and she slowly shuffled back to her seat.

Ida moved close enough to rub her hand across her student's hair. "Can you tell us why you feel I don't like you?"

"You never let me do fun stuff."

"Like what?" The older students had resumed writing, and the younger ones were drawing peaceably.

"I told you I could help you teach the little kids. All you ever let me do is stupid math pages."

Ida knelt so she could look into Nettie's eyes. "I appreciate your wanting to help me, Nettie. But you need to learn more before you can really help me."

"I already know how to read. I can read Jed's books."
Tears trembled at the edges of Nettie's eyes.

"I know you can, and that's important. But you also need
to know how to write neatly and how to add and subtract,
multiply and divide."

"But I hate math!"

Ida hugged her close. "I can understand that. I hated math,
too. But my mother always used to tell me that if I only did
the things I wanted to do, I'd grow up lazy and good for nothing. You don't want to be lazy, do you?"

Nettie shrugged, which Ida took for as much agreement as
she would get out of the strong-willed girl.

"How about if we start the math time test over again? Whoever does all the sums correctly can have fifteen extra minutes of recess."

By the end of the day, Ida felt completely worn out. Friday
contained no major confrontations, but she still felt frazzled.
That evening, Ken came for a visit and presented her with a
box of fresh carnations.

"Where did you get such gorgeous flowers?"

He grinned, obviously pleased with himself. "Father had
to go to the city this week and I asked him to bring them
back."

"They're marvelous. Lucy, come smell." The reds and
pinks along with their sweet fragrance lifted her spirits.

Lucy sniffed appreciatively. "They are lovely, Mr.
Danielson. How about if I put them in a bowl of water for
you, Ida, and I can bring you each a cup of hot cocoa in the
sitting room?"

"Thanks, Lucy." Ida impulsively hugged the older woman,
then led Ken to the little used room down the hall from the
kitchen. Several chairs covered in fancy material sat against
the walls, with a small, low table in the center of the room.

Ken held a chair for Ida, then chose one beside her for himself.

"I've been doing more thinking for the house, and wanted to get your opinion. I'd like to make it three stories, with the master suite taking up the entire second floor, and the children's rooms on the third floor. There should probably also be a room up there for a nanny. What do you think?"

Again Ida felt seized by a fairy-tale world. "It sounds like a house any woman would love. Where would you put the kitchen?"

"I thought of putting it in a wing off the ground floor so it wouldn't heat up the main part of the house during the summer. The wing would also have a couple of rooms in it for the cook/housekeeper."

"It sounds unbelievably luxurious." She permitted herself only a small smile lest she burst out laughing.

"Only the best for my wife, I say. What do you think of a summer honeymoon?" Apparently this scheme was no fairy tale to him.

She wondered how to detach herself gracefully. "Wouldn't you want to be engaged before you started planning your honeymoon? Your wife-to-be might have her own ideas."

Fortunately, Lucy arrived at that moment with the hot cocoa. The expression on Ken's face told Ida he hadn't even considered the possibility of his future wife not agreeing wholeheartedly with his plans. She sent an appealing message to Lucy, who interpreted it correctly.

"I'll just trot back to the kitchen for the popcorn, and join you two in a moment."

Ken's expression turned mildly sulky until Lucy returned and inquired, "Did I hear you say something about building your own house, Mr. Danielson?"

The opportunity to talk about his pet project cheered him

up immediately. "Yes, ma'am. I won't do the actual building, but I'm planning to design it myself."

Lucy listened attentively as he described various features, including rooms for the live-in help. To Ida's amazement, she also made suggestions.

"I'd think you'd want at least four bedrooms for the children, wouldn't you?"

Ken pondered for a moment. "That seems about right. Two boys and two girls would make a nice family."

"Since you'd have all that space on the second floor, would you build separate dressing rooms? I'd think it incredible luxury to have his and her dressing rooms, one on each side of the bedroom. You know, nice big rooms, each with a couple of chairs, maybe even a single bed in case one of you is ill."

Ida could see Ken visualizing the layout. "I hadn't thought about that."

"If you'll pardon an old lady's opinion, nothing wins a woman's heart like having her own space within a large master bedroom. If you plan it right, you could even have both dressing rooms open onto a common sitting room. Wouldn't that be lovely, Ida? A private sitting room off the master bedroom?"

Ken looked expectantly at Ida, who shrugged, feeling as though the conversation were running away from her. "I wouldn't know. I shared a room with Mother all my life. I've never even imagined the kind of luxury you're talking about." She listened to the two of them continue the discussion. Lucy's kind heart would never make fun of Ken. Why, then, did she embellish his notions?

Ken carefully stood to leave fifty-five minutes after he arrived. "Thank you for a lovely evening, Miss Thomas and Mrs. Barry. I've enjoyed your company."

"Thank you for the flowers," Ida replied, relieved she didn't have to offer any more opinions.

Lucy closed the front door behind him and turned to Ida with twinkling eyes. "I don't believe him! He left right on time, too."

"What do you mean?"

"In fancy places where life is more formal than it is here, a man who spends any more than an hour in a young lady's home is considered to be taking unfair advantage. You have to admit, his manners are flattering."

Sniffing her flowers again, Ida nodded. "I never dreamed I'd get flowers like this from anyone, especially here on the edge of nowhere."

"Wealth has its advantages, dear." Lucy's eyes sparkled again.

"But why did you encourage him in there? You know I'm not interested!" Ida heard an unfamiliar edge of hysteria creep into her voice.

Lucy wrapped a comforting arm around her. "I'm sure my encouragement, as you call it, isn't going to make him think you're serious. He wanted to talk about his house, so that's what we talked about. I didn't think it would hurt you to hear how his wife will be taken care of."

"Like some bird in a fancy cage with nothing to do. Did you hear him? A housekeeper to do all the cooking and cleaning and a nanny to take care of the children. What's the use of having a family if you don't care for them yourself?"

Lucy turned Ida so they could look into each other's eyes. "I'm glad to hear you say it. I wouldn't worry about Ken if I were you. He'll have a new project planned by Christmas, and this one will be forgotten."

Ida sighed. "I just hope he doesn't get seriously interested in me. About an hour at a time is all I can take of him."

"How about getting a good night's sleep? I'm sure this

won't look nearly so serious in the morning." Lucy hugged her and gently pushed her toward her bedroom.

But as Ida tossed on her bed that night, it wasn't Ken, his flowers, or his house that kept her awake. No matter what else she tried to think of, she couldn't free herself from Timothy and Ruth's sadness. This made the third consecutive night their grief-filled eyes had interrupted her sleep. She awoke Saturday morning, listless and weary. After lunch dishes had been washed and put away, Lucy poured the inevitable cups of tea and seated herself across the table from where Ida sat staring into space.

"You haven't been yourself for a couple of days. Is it Mr. Danielson?"

Ida sipped her tea, made from raspberry leaves, one of her favorites. "It's Ruth and her father."

"What about them?"

"I met Mr. McEvan on Wednesday. Phillip introduced me to him and Greg. Lucy, I've never seen so much sadness in a person. It's more than just grief. It's like he's given up hope of ever being happy again. And Ruth's the same way. It makes me wish Mother were here. She'd know what to do."

Lucy reached across the table to place her hands on Ida's arms. "You can't fix everyone's problems, dear girl. I know you want to help Ruth, but sometimes we have to let time do what we can't."

"But it's like they're locked behind a wall. How does a person get through?"

"Maybe if I tell you a bit of my story, you'll understand. Do you mind?"

The tone of her voice made Ida feel as though she were about to discover something well aged and precious. "Not at all."

"Kelvin Spencer and I were married in England when I

was just sixteen. He was personable, good looking, and reasonably wealthy. We adored each other in the way only very young newlyweds can. Two years later Kelvin Jr. was born, and Lionel a year after that. Kelvin Sr. did his best to protect me from anything unpleasant, other than childbirth, which he couldn't do much about. Nothing prepared me for losing him in 1914 at the beginning of the Great War. We would have been married fifteen years the day after I received the news. I simply went to pieces inside. We had sent the boys to live with their grandmother in the country before Kelvin left, so I didn't even have them to think about.

"Of course, nobody around me knew how bad I was. Kelvin and I had attended a wonderful little church ever since we were youngsters, and I worked hard to keep up the front I felt they expected. Many people told me how much they admired my strength. Little did they know how angry I was at God. Eleven months later, I volunteered as a WAC and got sent to France. Everybody thought I was so brave and patriotic. I actually hoped to be sent to the front so I'd be killed, too. I just got worse. Seeing all those truly brave young men getting killed or maimed increased my bitterness. Where was the good God I'd been taught about?

"Then one night in early 1916, two truckloads of us were on our way to the coast to be shipped back to Britain for reassignment. The other truck got blown to bits. I was hit on the head, and woke up in a British hospital unable to remember who or where I was. Gradually, it all came back to me, and with it my anger at God. By now the list of reasons for my anger had grown to an incredible length. One day, as I reviewed the list, I began to have thoughts like I'd never had before. I can still remember them like they came yesterday. The first one was, if God wasn't the loving God I'd thought He was, who lied? That troubled me for days. Since I was too weak to get out of bed, I had no way of running from the question. God says about Himself that He cannot lie. That meant my understanding of Him must have been warped. Eventually I asked the nurses for a Bible and began reading at random, searching for clues as to Who God really is. No matter where I read, I found myself confronted with God's compassion. At the same time, I saw innumerable instances of His allowing situations that seemed to be inexplicable in light of His love. It was the book of Job that pulled the two concepts together for me. God doesn't make sense to me because He is God. His love and His sovereignty at times seem totally unrelated. But if I could understand Him completely, He wouldn't be God. He'd be a construction of my own imagination.

"That's when I began learning about faith, the ability to trust Him even when He isn't making sense. It means refusing to give up on what He says about Himself, knowing that He cannot lie. About the time I'd made peace with Him, I was declared well enough to be sent out again. I had plenty of days where it would have been easier to retreat into anger, but God Himself had planted the seed of faith in me. I knew if I didn't choose to trust Him, I'd lose my sanity. Six months before the war ended, I met a Canadian soldier named William Barry, and Lionel and I followed him to the Peace Country.

"Five years later, influenza took him, too. This time faith carried me through the grief. It made all the difference."

The crackling of the fire in the cookstove made the only sound in the kitchen for several minutes. Ida finally found her voice. "Mother used to say, 'God's bigger than I am, so I just have to assume He knows what He's doing'."

Lucy nodded with understanding. "A lot of people think faith means admitting God caused my husbands to die, or

your parents, or Timothy McEvan's family. I don't believe
He arranges for these things to happen. I do believe, though,
they happen within His control, and only He can explain the
whys. I can't base my love for Him on knowing why."

"But how does that help me with Ruth?"

"Faith allows you to let God do the healing, even when it
looks like He's doing nothing."

"I just wish I could do something. I can't even sleep at
night from thinking about them."

"God could be trying to give you an assignment. Maybe
all they need is someone who loves them enough to keep praying for them."

Ida thought immediately of Theo's disclosures the week
before. She had her own grief to cope with. Perhaps that
would help her reach Ruth. But why would God ask her to
care about Timothy McEvan's sorrow as well?

seven

Carnations were only the first in Ken's series of unbelievable gifts. The next week, a massive box of chocolates arrived in the mail, with a tag bearing the words, "Regards, Ken Danielson" on the inside. Then a complete set of Jane Austen's writings.

Even Mr. Carey noticed during Sunday morning breakfast. "A body would think you wimen wuz settin' up your own store, the way things are piling up around here. At least there ain't any more of them smelly flowers."

Lucy just smiled sweetly at him. "Some men know how to give women something other than complaints. By the way, Mr. Carey, I haven't mentioned church to you for two whole months now. Care to go with us this morning?"

For once he didn't have an immediate answer. Lucy's eyes had begun to gleam with triumph when he coughed slightly. "I dunno. Working out in the chilly wind seems to be givin' me a bit of a head cold. Think I'd best stay inside today."

Ida choked on her pancakes. The ongoing debate between the two always amused her, but this morning both were in rare form.

"Chilly wind, my eye!" Lucy sputtered. "We've had the warmest autumn this year we've had in a long time. Tomorrow's the first of December, and it's just barely cold enough to keep the snow from melting. You're just looking for an excuse not to come."

"Could be right," Mr. Carey allowed, pushing himself back from the table. The click of his bedroom door ended the conversation.

Lucy stood in the middle of the kitchen, hands on hips, watching him go. "That man! Some days I think he says things just to get me riled."

"Could be right," Ida echoed, trying not to chuckle.

Lucy whirled to face her. "Whose side are you on, anyway?" Ida smirked, then both women laughed aloud.

"I guess it's God's job to get hold of him, not mine," Lucy muttered, clearing the table. "I just wish He'd let me help."

"I know what you mean." Ida put the salt and pepper shakers in the cupboard.

"How's Ruth doing?" A stack of clean dishes grew rapidly beside Lucy's dishpan.

"She talks to me a little more, as in greets me in the morning and says goodbye in the afternoon. She still looks incredibly sad, though."

"God seems to delight in doing things the slow way. I guess that teaches us more about trust. Remember, it took Him thirty years to give Abraham a son."

Ida meditated on the events of Abraham's life as they drove to the farm for church. Could she be as patient while waiting for God to bring relief to this student for whom she'd come to care so deeply?

Doug Pierce gave the sermon that morning, using Hebrews 10:36 as his text. *For ye have need of patience, that, after ye have done the will of God, ye might receive the promise.* Ida sat straight up in her chair as soon as she heard the verse. It was as if Doug had been listening to her thoughts this morning. "Sometimes God gives us concerns we don't understand," he said. "It may be a neighbor who doesn't know Him yet, or a dream for our own lives. He lets us know what he wants to accomplish, then seems to go completely silent. Sometimes everything in the world goes contrary to the dream we feel we received from Him. That's when faith becomes crucial. If we can believe He meant what He said, regardless of what circumstances look like, we bring joy to Him. Look with me at Luke chapter 22, verse 32. Jesus tells Peter, 'But I have prayed for thee, that thy faith fail not: and when thou art converted, strengthen thy brethren.' As an illustration, I'd like to tell you a bit of our family's story." The group was seated in an informal circle. Doug had remained seated while he talked, and he reached for Cynthia's hand as he closed his Bible.

"Most of you know we lost three babies after Theodore was born. You probably don't know that each of those babies seemed like an answer to prayer. When we were first married, a doctor had told us Cynthia wouldn't be able to have children. Theo was our first miracle, and we'd asked God for one more so he wouldn't have to grow up an only child. For the first year after he was born, it seemed like every time we opened our Bibles, we found a reference to God giving children. We wrote each passage down and kept praying. After a year or so, we stopped getting such dramatic reassurance. We reviewed the early promises and kept praying. Four years passed before another little one appeared. She lived less than an hour. I was ready to give up on God at that point, but my wife wouldn't let me. 'God doesn't lie,' she'd say. 'We just have to wait some more.' Two years later, another baby died. Then another three years later. When I'd get discouraged, Cynthia would remind me of the promises. When the grief would get too much for her, I'd feel confident God would come through.

"Theodore grew up with our hope and disappointments. In the year before Sara was born, it seemed he had more faith than both his parents. We were almost afraid to hope when we learned another baby was on the way. Somehow Theo was positive this would be our 'promise baby' as he called it. Sure enough, little Sara was born healthy, and she's been a joy to us ever since. When you're wondering if God's really there, take a look at my family. We've seen Him do the impossible, and we want to strengthen your faith."

Through her tears, Ida noticed Ruth in a corner wiping her eyes. She quietly moved to put her arm around the girl. "Are you okay?"

Ruth tried unsuccessfully to stop crying, then turned and buried her face in Ida's shoulder, sobs shaking her. Ida held her close. Gradually Ruth was able to speak. "Why did God do that for them but He killed my mother and brothers?"

Her grief caused Ida's eyes to overflow. "I don't know why He let it happen, honey, but He wasn't the one who killed them. The river did that."

Ruth sobbed some more. "If I hadn't been there, it wouldn't have happened."

"What do you mean?" Ida rubbed her back gently. The rest of the group had moved to the table for lunch, except for Theo, who stood watching them from a distance.

"If I hadn't been there, the raft wouldn't have been too heavy."

"Ruthie," the endearment came naturally. "We don't know that. I know little about what happened, but I don't think we'll ever be sure why it happened. Just like I don't know why God let my daddy be killed in the war or my mother get sick and die last spring."

Ruth pulled back to look at Ida. "Your mother died, too?" Little hiccups still shook her. "And your dad?"

Ida nodded. "That's why I came here. I had to find a job because I was all alone."

"Do you miss them all the time?"

"Yes." She had to wipe away more tears.

Tears still ran down Ruth's cheeks, too. "Daniel was my twin brother, my best friend. We told each other everything. I saw the log hit him and he disappeared. I was too far away to do anything. Mama tried to hold Sam and Benjamin up, but the river just carried all of them away. I was holding Greg, so I couldn't swim to help her, either."

"But you did save Greggy." Ida used her handkerchief to wipe Ruth's face.

"I know, and I wish I could feel grateful, but I don't. Most times, I'd rather have Mama and Daniel here than Greg. And then I feel so guilty for that, too." She sobbed into Ida's shoulder some more.

"Honey, feeling guilty won't bring your mama or your brother back. I'm sure you did all you could."

"But why didn't God let it be enough? Why Daniel instead of Greg?"

Ida wished she had an easy answer. "I don't know, Ruthie. It's one of those hard questions only God knows the answer to."

"Sometimes I hate Him, too." The words were whispered into Ida's collar.

"That's all right. He can handle it. One day, you'll be ready to love Him again, and He'll be waiting for you."

"Why would He care about me? I've said such awful things to Him when nobody else can hear." Ruth looked into Ida's eyes questioningly.

Ida hoped the conviction of her soul came through in her voice. "He loves you just because you're you."

"It's just so hard. I feel like there's nobody in the world who understands. You were a grown lady when your mama died."

"Maybe it seems that way to you. Sometimes I still feel like a little girl. Some nights, I miss her so badly, I can't help crying into my pillow."

Ruth studied Ida's face for a long moment, then wiped her eyes again.

"Ruth, you have another friend, someone else who understands a little bit."

Her eyebrows puckered. "Who?"

"Theodore. Remember what his dad said?"

"Yeah." She plucked at the frayed edges of her sleeves. "I guess so. But you heard what his dad said. He'd think I was awful for hating God."

"I doubt that. You should talk to him some time."

"Maybe." Ruth considered it. "But you won't tell anyone what I said. Please?"

"Of course not. I hope you'll come to me if you need to talk again. I can't say I understand, but I'd like to listen. Holding it all in just makes you feel worse."

She nodded. "I know. I already feel better than I have since the river. I just wish I didn't miss them so badly."

Ida pulled her into a hug. "I know. Believe me, I know. But Mrs. Barry says it gets easier after awhile. How about if we go see how much lunch is left?"

"I hope I don't look too awful."

Ida smiled and took her hand. "I'm sure no one will mind."

They filled their plates, finding seats a little away from the rest of the group, who gave Ida reassuring glances, but didn't ask any questions. Theo quietly sat beside Ruth.

Ken waited until they'd finished eating before approaching Ida. "Would you go for a sleigh ride with me this afternoon? I brought my dad's sleigh in case you said yes."

She felt too emotionally drained to cope with him. Then a look at Ruth's face gave her an idea. Maybe an hour or so looking at the countryside would help them both collect themselves after the storm. She felt badly for using Ken, but it would be for a good cause. "That sounds like a lovely idea. Would you mind if Ruth comes, too?"

His eyes told her he minded very much, but good manners asserted themselves. "Of course not. I'd be flattered to have two lovely ladies with me."

Theo rolled his eyes, bringing a faint smile to Ruth's lips. "Thanks, Miss Thomas," he whispered, as he took Ida's plate, then Ruth's.

"Let's go then. Your dad won't mind?" She felt compelled to ask.

Ruth shook her head. "He always cooks lunch for him and the boys on Sunday afternoons, and they take long naps."

Ida quickly told Lucy where they were going. "I'll try to be back in about an hour."

"Is Ruth all right?"

The smile threatened to split her face. "I think she's on her way."

Lucy closed her eyes. "Thank the Lord."

"You said it." Ida hurried out to the sleigh where Ruth was already seated. Ken stood waiting to help her in. She noticed he'd maneuvered things to have her beside him. Three would be a tight fit. She'd have preferred Ruth between them, but oh well. Just an hour wouldn't hurt her. And it might help Ruth a lot.

Snow blanketed everything in sight, including hay stooks. The hills in the distance displayed varying shades of gray and white, laced with the black of bare tree branches.

"Looks like winter's here for good," Ken commented companionably.

"What's it like here?" Ida asked, mostly to make conversation.

Ruth answered emphatically. "Cold."

"It probably seems colder out on the farm." Ken's

voice conveyed just a touch of superiority. "In town, we have sleighing parties, music nights, and plenty of activities to keep us from noticing the cold."

Ida wondered if this had been such a good idea. Ken apparently didn't mind Ruth's presence as long as she kept quiet. She looked over at Ruth, who seemed unaware of Ken's attitude. Well, the girl needed Ida's company this afternoon, and Ken would just have to put up with it. "What does your family do in the wintertime, Ruth?"

"Just the usual stuff. Dad usually works out in the barn when I'm home to watch the boys. Once I've done everything that needs doing, it's time for bed." Ruth sighed, a tired woman kind of sigh.

Lord, why was it necessary to turn a child into an old woman? This girl should be excited about sledding, and popcorn by the fire, and Christmas. On the edges of the thought came Mother's voice. "Without challenges, you'd be lazy and good for nothing." *Isn't this challenge a little much for a teenage girl? I'm sorry, Lord. I choose to trust you, since I can't understand.*

Ruth grabbed Ida's arm. "Oh, look! There's a moose over there."

Ida's gaze followed the line of Ruth's arm and pointing finger. "Ken, would you stop the sleigh for a moment?"

He gave her a long-suffering look, but halted the horses.

In a patch of willows stood the strangest looking animal Ida had ever seen. His snout was as broad as his forehead, though the center of his face was tapered like an hourglass. Long ears flopped on either side of his head. Large flat antlers made him look top-heavy in spite of the long, deep-chested body behind and below them. Long, skinny legs with bulbous knees held the animal up. "Those legs look too awkward to be real," Ida whispered.

"Can we leave now before he decides to charge at us?" Ken asked impatiently, clucking to the horses without waiting for a reply.

"They don't charge unless you get between a mother and her calf. The males only charge at each other during mating season," Ruth informed Ida quietly. Her whisper held a wealth of disdain for this city man who was frightened of wild animals.

"Ruth, would you like to come home with me for supper?" Ida asked the question specifically so Ken wouldn't feel invited.

"How would I let my dad know?"

Relieved Ruth didn't immediately decline, she quickly improvised. "We'll have to pass your farm on the way back. I'm sure Mr. Danielson wouldn't mind stopping for a moment. I'll even go in and ask for you." She felt Ken stiffen beside her, but didn't care. His childishness had become tiresome.

Ruth looked directly at her for the first time since they'd left Spencers. "If he doesn't mind, I'd like that."

Mr. McEvan had just closed the barn door when they pulled into the farm yard. Ida noticed how clean and tidy everything looked. "Ken, I'd like to get out, please."

He clambered off the sleigh and helped her to her feet.

"Mr. McEvan?"

"Yeah?" Though he didn't smile, he didn't sound disgruntled by their presence.

Since he hadn't seemed to recognize her, she decided an introduction would be the best first move. "I'm Ida Thomas, Ruth and Phillip's teacher."

"Phillip introduced us awhile back." Again, those deeply pained blue eyes arrested her attention.

"I wasn't sure if you remembered." She tried to smile.

"Ruth accompanied Mr. Danielson and me on a ride after church today, and I was wondering if you'd mind if I took her home with me for dinner. Mrs. Barry and I will bring her back before it gets too late."

He looked at his daughter, who nodded. "Sounds okay. I guess I don't have to tell you she has school tomorrow." From another man, the comment would have sounded like a good joke.

"Thank you, sir. I'll take good care of her."

He touched his hat brim and proceeded toward the house without a look back.

Ken stayed silent the rest of the way into town and helped them out of the sleigh without a word. He looked like one of Ida's first-graders in a pout as he drove off.

"I guess I kinda ruined your drive," Ruth commented.

"Not mine," Ida assured her. "I invited you, remember?"

"Yeah, but your beau wasn't too happy."

"He's not my beau. Lucy, I brought a guest."

Never happier than when fussing over company, Lucy welcomed Ruth warmly. "I'm glad to see you, child. I hope you'll pardon Mr. Carey's manners. He's had a bad cold today, so he's too wobbly in the knees to stand. Mr. Carey, this young lady is Ruth McEvan, one of Ida's students."

He nodded at Ruth before taking another loud slurp of his coffee. "Done tole you, Miz Barry, you're too late to try reformin' me."

"I wouldn't think of reforming you, Mr. Carey," Lucy shot back. "God's the one who can do that."

"Now don't start preachin' at me, woman. If I'd huv wanted a sermon, I'd huv gone to church." He winked at Ruth, whose eyes had gone round at their bickering.

"And it wouldn't have harmed you a bit. Ida, would you mind showing Ruth around? I have this pie crust almost ready to roll."

Ida gave her the tour, ending at her own room. Ruth went straight to the window, which showed a similar panorama as it had at the old location. "What a beautiful view!"

"I know. I fell in love with it first thing, even though it always makes me think of my mother."

Ruth turned to face her. "Why?"

"The last few years, we lived in an apartment that had only tiny windows which faced another building. Mother always wished we could have had a prettier view."

"I wish I could have met your mother." She trailed her fingers across the edge of Ida's desk.

"And I wish I could have met yours."

Ruth blinked a couple of times, but didn't break down. "I do too, and Daniel." After a long pause she continued. "I also wish my dad would cry."

"Why is that?" Ida felt like someone had punched her in the stomach. She could picture the shattered blue gaze without trying.

"Because it helps. I always thought it would make me feel worse if I cried, so I kept it all tight inside me. Then when Mr. Pierce was talking, I looked at you crying and I couldn't help myself. I tried to stop. I felt réally embarrassed, then you hugged me and I had to cry harder. I'm glad you were there."

Ida pulled her down so they could sit side by side on the bed. "Ruthie, you've had more sadness in your life than a lot of people ever have. My mother always used to say God gave us tears to keep us cleaned out inside. If you keep the tears in, it just makes you hurt worse."

"I know that now, and I wish my Dad did." Ruth laid her head against Ida's shoulder.

"May I tell you something else?"

"Yes, ma'am."

She put her arm around Ruth's skinny shoulders. "You're going to feel like crying more before you're better. Will you promise me you won't try to keep it back? Even if you're at school and need to go for a walk so you can cry, please tell me."

Ruth sniffed. "I just feel like I'm going to cry for the rest of my life."

"You won't. I promise. Some days I feel like that too, but Mrs. Barry says it gets better."

Ruth raised her head with a smile. "She's a nice lady, isn't she?"

"She's wonderful. I'll bet if we go out there now, she'll offer us both some tea. Shall we do it?"

"But first," Ruth hesitated. "Would you mind praying that my Dad'll cry, too? He been so sad and mad, like me, only he doesn't have anybody to talk to."

Ida placed her hands over Ruth's. "I'll do that, if you'll promise you'll let yourself cry when you feel like it." Only she knew she couldn't have stopped praying for Timothy McEvan if she'd wanted to.

They'd barely opened the bedroom door when Lucy held a chair out from the table. "Sit here, Ruth. Would you like a cup of tea?"

Ruth's eyes twinkled at Ida briefly. "Yes, please."

Ruth and Ida managed few words during supper. Ida suspected Lucy kept goading Mr. Carey just to entertain their guest. "I suppose that cold of yours has your appetite down to normal size, so I'll just give you a single slice of roast."

He seemed to warm to an audience as well. "Whatcha tryin' to do, starve me? I'll let you know if I'm not hungry."

"That'll be the day. I'd probably think you were dying."

"Then you wouldn't have anybody to pick on. Mind if I eat now?"

A grin flitted across Ruth's face just before Lucy turned to her. "Are you getting enough? Mr. Carey tends to clean the dishes out before visitors get a fair chance."

"I have plenty, thank you." Obviously Ruth's mother had trained her well in their few years together. Once the meal was over, she quietly helped clear the table.

To Ida's surprise, Lucy handed the girl a dish towel. "If you don't mind helping me, dear, we'll get this place cleaned up in a trice." She carefully drew the girl out as they worked, asking questions about recipes she used and her brothers' food preferences. After dishes were done, she made tea, which she served in fine china cups Ida hadn't seen before.

Before they took Ruth home, Lucy took one of her hands and one of Ida's, then bowed her head. Ruth and Ida made the circle complete as they listened to a prayer that brought an almost tangible feeling of comfort into the room. Though Ruth couldn't have known, Ida knew the older woman was praying from her own experiences of bereavement. Doug Pierce had been right. Faith that had been severely tested became a source of strength for others in need.

eight

School brought more challenges on Tuesday. Another thick layer of snow had fallen during the night. Its undisturbed whiteness lay just beyond the windows, inviting Ida's students to come out and play in it. She gave them extra long breaks at recess and lunch, hoping to burn off some of their energy. Thankfully, the Young Lionel and Jed had come today. Their presence always seemed to stabilize the younger ones. Jim, who missed more school than any of them, was absent today as well. Ida had a hunch education didn't carry the same priority with him or his parents as the farm. So be it. Many of the farmers in the area knew little more than how to read, write, and add. They still took care of their families well and contributed to the well-being of the community.

By afternoon recess, Ida realized further studies were a lost cause. Maybe this was the right time to introduce an idea she'd been toying with since Moving Day. She insisted everyone be seated, then waited for Michael and David to finish their whispered conversation.

"What does snow make you think of?" She smiled at their ruby-cheeked faces, eyes sparkling with the joy of a new season.

Without putting her hand up, Nettie suggested, "Snow angels." The school yard gave mute evidence of this being on more than one child's mind.

"Good. How about if we take turns making suggestions? Put your hand up if you have an idea, and I'll make sure everyone gets a chance. Next?"

Clara shyly suggested hot chocolate. Michael thought of snowball fights. Tommy mentioned toboggan rides, and Young Lionel hockey games. This made Patricia think of skating on the river. Just when Ida thought they'd never make the suggestion she wanted, Karin whispered, "Christmas." Popcorn, candy, presents, Christmas trees, carols—the barrage of resulting ideas was deafening.

Ida laughed and held up her hands for silence. "Wait just a minute. I can't hear if everyone talks at once." She wrote the ideas down on the chalk board until interest started dwindling. Then she asked, "Have you ever put on a Christmas concert?"

Total silence reigned for a minute, then bedlam erupted. It seemed everyone had a question. Ida answered them as quickly as she could. Yes, a play would be fun. Yes, everyone would get a part in the concert. Even the youngest ones, too, Phillip. The parents would probably help with the costumes and props, although if Jed and Young Lionel wanted to help there, too, that would be fine. When asked what kind of play they'd do, Ida threw the question back at them. "What kind do you want to do?" To her surprise, most of them wanted to do a Nativity play. In a way, it was a relief. The story was familiar, so the lines wouldn't be hard to learn. But what would she do to make this concert different from the average? Maybe Lucy would have some ideas.

They spent the rest of the afternoon discussing their project. To her amazement, everyone agreed Patricia would make the best Mary. "She's so pretty and quiet," Nettie explained. The six-year-olds all wanted to be shepherds, and Nettie wanted to be Herod. Ida would have to figure out a way to redirect that ambition.

When school let out, she had to resist the urge to collapse at her desk for a quick nap before heading home. She leaned her head back as far as she could, stretching out the tight neck muscles. When she straightened up again, Ruth was standing just inside the door. Ida smiled at her reassuringly. Since their talk on Sunday, Ruth had seemed to retreat into herself, though Ida had noticed her talking to Theo during recesses. Her eyes had seemed a bit brighter, as well, but she'd made no more gestures of friendship to Ida.

The teenager approached Ida's desk hesitantly. "Are you busy?"

"No, I'm actually too tired to get anything done right now. Sit here, if you'd like." She patted the edge of her desk.

Ruth smiled shyly. "The kids were ornery today, weren't they?"

Ida nodded, pleased she'd noticed anything beyond herself.

"I think your idea of a Christmas concert is wonderful." Ruth studied her hands, then continued in a rush. "But what I really wanted to tell you is thanks for Sunday. I didn't say anything before because I didn't want the other kids to think I'm trying to be teacher's pet or anything. But I'm feeling lots better than I have in a long time. And when I miss my mother or Daniel so much I think I'm going to scream, I remember what you said about it not always being like this." Tears trembled on her lashes when she looked back up at Ida.

Ida felt a lump in her own throat. This girl's pain was so similar and yet so much more devastating than her own. At least she seemed willing to talk. "May I show you something, Ruth?" She lifted her cape off the hook near the blackboard and tucked it around the girl's shoulders. "This is the last garment my mother ever made for me."

"Did your mother make all your clothes?" Ruth whispered, running her hands over the soft wool.

Ida nodded. "She wanted to make sure I had pretty things

to help me find a job after she was gone."

"My mother didn't have time to do anything for me before . . ." she couldn't continue.

"I know, Ruth." Ida dared to enfold her in a hug. "That's why I thought it might help if I shared some of the special things my mother did for me. I have a feeling your mother would have done the same, if she'd known what was going to happen."

"If we'd known, we wouldn't have let it happen." With a quick gesture, Ruth angrily flung Ida's cape to the floor.

Ida didn't stoop to pick it up, lest she break eye contact. "I know."

"No, you don't." Like a summer thunderstorm, the girl's anger seemed to rumble out of nowhere. "You say you do, but you don't. My mother left me nothing. Nothing, do you hear? Nothing except nightmares of watching her drown. It wasn't your twin brother that drowned with her, it was mine. Mine." A sob cut off her words, but she wasn't finished. "All I have left are two little brothers who can't remember anything, and a dad who never even looks at me anymore. You can't know." She ran out, slamming the door behind her.

Ida stooped to retrieve the cape. How had she destroyed the budding friendship so quickly? She made sure the fire in the small stove was down to embers, bundled herself up, and started home. Thankfully, Misty seemed to know the way, so Ida could let her thoughts tumble at will. Once the animal was stabled and rubbed down and the saddle hung in its place, she wandered absently into the house. Somehow, Ruth's outburst had returned her healing heart to its previous painfully wounded condition. The hurt went too deep for tears.

"Ida, honey. Whatever is the trouble?" Lucy took one look at the teacher's troubled face and began fussing around her, unbuttoning her cape, pushing her into a chair, placing a steaming cup of tea before her. "You look done in."

As unemotionally as she could, Ida related the events of her day. "I just don't know what I did wrong, Lucy. I thought she was doing so well."

Lucy didn't demean Ida's pain with an immediate answer. Only the scrunch of her knife against the potatoes she peeled and the crackling wood in the stove broke the long silence. Eventually, she faced Ida and asked almost in a whisper, "How often did you get angry before your mother died?"

Remembering her outbursts still brought guilt. Ida recalled her unrelenting rage, particularly in the early days of her mother's illness. "More often than I'd like to remember."

"Of course you did, child. It's part of grief. You felt it beforehand because you knew what was coming. Young Ruth feels it now because she didn't."

"But it was like she blamed me." Even as she said the words, she remembered accusing her own mother. She'd known at the time her mother wasn't to blame, but she couldn't seem to help herself.

Lucy's kindly gaze seemed to perceive Ida's thoughts. She only suggested, "Why don't you take a bit of a rest before supper?"

By the time Ken arrived later in the evening for his inevitable visit, Ida felt more like herself. Maybe Ruth had simply reacted as Ida herself had done not so long ago. Ken's offering of another bunch of carnations helped also. She found herself excitedly discussing the Christmas concert with him and Lucy. "I'm not sure how we're going to make a Nativity play into something which won't bore the parents, but at least my students are enthusiastic about it."

"Could I lend some help building backdrops?"

Ken's offer almost stunned Ida into speechlessness. "I'll be grateful for any help I can get. How about if I let you know when we've decided what we need?"

"Sounds good." Ken beamed at her.

Ida looked at Lucy, wondering at his unusual demeanour. Lucy gave a slight shrug while saying, "Are you interested in an old lady's suggestion for your concert?"

"Sure!"

"Why not use the Nativity play as a background for each of the students to do some kind of performance? You could have the little ones sing a song. Maybe the older ones would like to do a Christmas-type recitation. You could make these special bits something that relates to the difference Jesus can make in lives now."

Anticipation made Ida tingle all over. "And the ones who don't want to do something special can have parts in the play. You're a genius, Lucy!"

Ken shifted a bit in his chair while they planned, but he didn't try to change the subject. He laughed when Ida mentioned Nettie's comments. "Would she settle for being one of the three wise men? If you give her a poem to recite as well, that might keep her busy enough to forget about Herod."

"He might have an idea, there," Lucy offered as she left to answer a knock at the front door.

Ida could hear Lionel and Nina's familiar voices explaining they'd been out for a drive and just stopped in for a few moments. She noticed Ken studying her with an uncertain expression on his face. "What is it, Mr. Danielson?"

He grimaced. "I really wish you'd call me Ken, and I'd like to call you Ida. What I mean is ... uh ... well, actually ..." He cleared his throat, took a deep breath, and tried again. "Would you mind if I came courting?"

Ida had always hoped such a moment would fill her with a bubbly sort of delight. Right now, she only felt as though she were about to board a train for an unknown destination. She didn't want to hurt his feelings, but neither did she want to agree too quickly. "I don't know what to say, Ken." The use of his first name brought a sparkle of pleasure to his eyes. "I'm flattered, but I'd like time to think it over if you don't mind."

His suave polish gradually reasserted itself. "Of course. I'll be counting the minutes."

What for? she wanted to ask, but that would sound churlish. "Thanks for understanding."

He nodded and stood. "I need to leave now, but I'll see you on Sunday." He reached for her hand, which she tucked behind her back.

She let him out the front door, then joined the others at the kitchen table. Lucy took a clean cup and saucer out of the cupboard. "I've just been telling Lionel and Nina about your Christmas concert."

"It sounds marvelous to me," Nina declared, laying a hand on her rounded stomach. "Since I'm not too active these days, I'd be happy to help sew costumes, and I'm sure Kate would help, as well. She's a better seamstress than you'd think."

Lionel covered Nina's hand with his own. "I'll make sure my wife doesn't overdo."

"Oh, Lionel." Nina looked at her husband with affectionate exasperation. "A bit of sewing won't hurt me, especially since you insist on the kids doing most of the housework. Having babies has never given me any trouble."

"That's because I make sure you're taken care of." His firm comment closed that part of the discussion. "But Miss Thomas, do you think it would be possible to invite more than just parents to the concert?"

"Of course," Lucy interrupted. "Grandparents will be welcome too, or I'll know the reason why."

Lionel protested through the laughter, "That's not what I

meant, Mother. I'd like to see some of the townfolk come out, too."

"Would there be enough room in the school?" Ida couldn't envision the necessary space.

"I think there's an empty storeroom in the Co-op building. Lars might be able to get us permission to use it, if you'd like. A couple of us men could hammer together a sturdy stage, and I'm sure we could round up enough chairs."

The project had suddenly blossomed far past Ida's imaginings. "Do you think the children could handle performing in front of strangers?"

"Why not leave the decision with them?" Nina suggested. "Much as we'd like to show them off, if they're too shy, we'll respect that."

But when Ida mentioned the idea the next day, the class gave their resounding approval. Even Jim, who'd heard about the excitement and decided to check it out, thought it would be fun. "If we know the townfolk'll be there too, it'll make us work harder to do it right," he commented.

Nettie didn't like that. "We'll do it right anyway, Jim! We're not a bunch of babies, you know."

Recognizing family rivalry for what it was, Ida deftly changed the subject. "I have one other idea. I'd like to hear some of you sing Christmas songs, or recite Christmas poems, or something like that, if you want to."

"Can we pick our own?" Patricia wondered.

"I'd like to check them out first, but yes, I'd like you to pick what you want to do."

From there, the last hour of every school day was devoted to preparing for The Concert. The excitement even spilled over to the church gathering on Sunday. It took Lionel several tries to get everyone seated so the short service could begin. Just before he bowed his head for opening prayer,

Ruth McEvan slipped in, followed by her father and brothers.

Ida watched them out of the corner of her eye. The boys behaved well, though they kept trying to wave to her. Ruth often glanced her way, as well. But Timothy's face captured Ida's most frequent notice most. He seemed familiar with a church-like setting, but uncomfortable at the same time. As Lionel read from Psalm 91, Ida thought for sure Timothy would leave. But he stayed, and even joined the line for lunch, after Doug assured him there was plenty for everyone. "The ladies each bring enough for their families, plus a few more, and we always have leftovers. We'd love to have you." He clapped Timothy on the shoulder and ruffled Greg's hair. "I'll bet there's even a piece of chocolate cake over there your size, young man."

"Me, too?" Phillip wanted to know.

"If your dad says yes." Doug carefully handed the question over to Timothy, who nodded with a small smile and herded his troupe to the table.

"Miss Thomas." Ken startled her out of her preoccupation. When she looked at him, he lowered his voice conspiratorially. "I'd like to take you to my parents' place for lunch today, if you don't mind. My mother said you'd be welcome."

Ida had met his parents during one of her first weeks in town and saw them often when she and Lucy did their weekly shopping. It wasn't like she'd be eating with strangers, but for some reason she couldn't define, she didn't want to miss out on today's "family lunch" as they called it. "I appreciate the invitation, Ken, but I don't often get to visit with my students' parents in a group like this. I'd prefer to stay here."

His knitted eyebrows indicated his preferences weren't often crossed. But he quickly put on a smile. "I'll just go on myself, then. See you later this week."

Nothing dramatic happened or was discussed during the meal. Both Phillip and Tommy spilled their milk, Nettie tried to help herself to three pieces of cake, and Tabitha spent more time crawling under the table than eating. Ida noticed neither Timothy nor Ruth ate much, but at least they were there. Somehow it made her glad she'd stayed.

nine

Just a single day later, Ida glanced up from her work-covered desk. Though the other students played in the snow outside, Ruth hovered by the door with Theodore beside her. "Hello, you two."

Ruth's face turned pink, while Theodore nudged her arm. Ida could barely make out his whispered comment. "It's okay."

Ruth cleared her throat, a small, strangling sound. "Miss Thomas . . ." Her voice trailed off.

Ida kept her voice as gentle as possible. "How about coming next to my desk. It's hard to say anything across a room. Now what is it?"

"I'm just sorry." Once she found the courage to talk, Ruth kept her gaze locked on Ida's. "I didn't mean all those awful things I said. I know you miss your mother, too."

Ida stretched out her arms, letting Ruth choose whether or not to receive the hug. "I know you didn't mean it." She cradled the thin shoulders. "I said lots of terrible things to my mother when I found out how sick she was. It's hard to get used to being without them, isn't it?"

Ruth pulled back. "I didn't think you knew how to be not nice."

Ida chuckled. "I think everyone's born knowing how, Ruth. We just learn how to choose to be different."

"I was so scared to come talk to you."

"Why?"

"You'd been so nice to me ever since you came and then I

ruined it." She looked into Ida's face anxiously. "I wasn't really mad at you."

"Well, since we've talked it over, let's just pretend it never happened. Okay?"

The first real smile Ida had ever seen on Ruth's face touched the girl's eyes before turning up the edges of her mouth.

"Told you she'd be good about it," Theodore reminded his friend triumphantly. "Now you can stop worrying."

Ida handed Ruth the bell. "Would you call the others in, please?" As Theo held the door open for Ruth, Ida felt like the sun had come from behind a long-lasting cloud. Even Nettie's temper tantrum later in the afternoon couldn't mar her happiness.

On Friday, Theo came to school bearing fancy envelopes that he handed out at the end of the day to the oldest child of each family represented, with one left over for Ida. "We're having a toboggan party at our farm tomorrow afternoon, and everyone's invited. The paper in the envelopes will tell your parents everything." He looked at Ida. "Mother said to make sure Mrs. Barry knows she's welcome, too."

Ida had more fun than she dreamed possible. Bundled up in woolen socks and flannel petticoats beneath her heavy skirt, two heavy sweaters beneath her cape, a knitted hat, a similarly knitted scarf tied around her head and neck, and woolly mittens, she could hardly move. But as Lucy had said while digging the warm clothes out of a closet, "You can't have fun at a sledding party if you're cold."

Ida had wondered if people might think her too undignified if she participated in the sledding, but Lucy pooh-poohed that idea. "Nina'd be out there if it wouldn't give Lionel fits. You just have fun enough to include those of us who have to stay in by the fire."

Each of the children, including the older boys, insisted on

giving Teacher a ride. Before Ida had her fill of sledding, the older Lionel started a snowball fight with Doug Pierce that escalated into war. Those who had been surprised to see the entire McEvan family show up were further amazed when Timothy crammed snow down the back of Lionel's jacket. Doug had built a large bonfire at which the participants warmed themselves periodically. Before the younger children could get too tired, Cynthia called everyone inside for supper—steaming bowls of chili, hot buns fresh from the oven, and mugs of hot cocoa. Dirty dishes seemed to vanish, and someone started humming a familiar tune. Others filled in the words. Ida didn't notice when the songs changed to hymns, which the children appeared to know as well as the adults.

She did notice Timothy McEvan. He sat quietly while everyone chattered during supper. He didn't participate in the singing, though he seemed in no hurry to leave. During one of the hymns, she noticed the glint of moisture just above his beard.

A strange noise outside brought the singing to a halt. Doug hurried to the door. "Would you look at that?" he intoned.

When Ida could finally catch a glimpse through the bodies crowding around, she wondered if she was seeing right. Having lived in the city, she recognized a car when she saw it. It was the identity of the driver that amazed her, though she realized later it shouldn't have. Ken Danielson. "Is Miss Thomas in there?" he inquired, barely concealing his pride at the stir he caused.

The crush miraculously thinned, allowing her to get through. "Wherever did you get an automobile, Mr. Danielson?"

"We went to the city for it this week. Do you like it?"

What else could a person say at such a moment? If she could have been honest, she would have admitted that it seemed ill-mannered to flash such a purchase before farmers such as her friends who worked hard to keep food on the table and homes in good repair. But Ken would never understand that, and her friends would be embarrassed if she tried to explain it. She merely said, "It looks nice."

"Well, grab your coat and I'll take you home."

Ida felt intensely uncomfortable as she searched for her cape, sweaters, socks, hat, and scarf in the pile of winter clothing. Lucy quietly joined her. "All you'll need is your cape, which is right here. I'll bring the rest when I come."

"I feel like I'm breaking up the party." Ida searched Lucy's gaze for comfort.

It came in the form of a hug. "Nonsense. It's time to get the children home for bed, anyway. I'm sure not a soul here blames you."

Ida made sure she thanked Cynthia for the marvelous afternoon, then waded through a progression of hugs from her students. Ken stood just outside the door. *Strange that Doug hadn't invited him in. But then, where would one more person have fit?*

"At last. I thought I'd lost you forever in that crowd." He opened the passenger's side door with a flourish. She couldn't see the vehicle clearly in the dark, but she could feel the smooth seat coverings. A smell of newness surrounded her when he shut her door. After seating himself, he carefully maneuvered the car out of the driveway and turned onto the road heading away from town, the car's headlamps dimly illuminating the snow-covered trail ahead.

"I thought you were taking me home!" Ida protested.

"The long way," he explained, with a trace of smugness in his tone. "So what do you really think of my car?"

Ida tried to laugh. "It seems, oh, I guess a little extravagant. Although it's very nice," she hastened to reassure him.

"But that's what the Danielsons are all about. Luxuries

farmers can only dream about." His arrogance jarred her nerves.

"Farmers are the kind of people I work with every day, Ken."

"I know, and I admire you for it. I admire you for a lot of reasons."

What had taken over him? It seemed as though his manners had been just a veneer that now peeled off. She tried to pass it over with a joke. "Now, Ken, if you're going to embarrass me, I'll have to ask you to take me home."

His voice grew soft. "I'd never want to embarrass you, Ida. I've never met a woman like you. You're perfect."

Perfect for what? She chose another question. "How did you know where I was?"

He chuckled. "That old bird who lives at the boarding-house told me. He didn't seem too happy Mrs. Barry hadn't stayed around to cook his supper."

"Mr. Carey's always fussing about something." She said it affectionately, feeling a strange resentment at Ken's reference. *Was it possible he didn't see value in anyone other than those with whom he chose to associate?* She tried to make the question sound casual, a getting-acquainted kind of inquiry. "Who are your friends in this area?"

"In Dawson Creek?" He seemed to find the idea highly amusing. "I have just one, a beautiful, kind-hearted lady with gentle green eyes and soft-looking blond hair."

She hadn't expected that kind of response. "Do you have many friends, then?"

"Lots in the city. They're always coming up with something different to do. You wouldn't believe some of it."

Ida felt sure she wouldn't. How could fine, ordinary folk like Mr. and Mrs. Danielson have produced a son such as the young man with whom she now rode? Actually, the automobile

explained a lot of the problem. Overindulgence. It had ruined many children. "Shouldn't we be turning around? I
don't want to be out too late."

Silently, he backed and turned the car until they were facing back toward town. "I'm not going to quit trying, Ida."

She could think of no reply. They passed Pierces' driveway. Just before reaching the turnoff for the school, she noticed something strange by the side of the road. "What is
that?" She thought she recognized the figure standing beside
a wagon. "Ken, please stop." She barely waited for the car
to cease moving before she yanked her door open. "Mr.
McEvan, are you all right?"

"Miss Thomas? I thought you went home a long time ago."

She chose not to explain. "What happened? Are the children with you?"

"My horse seems to have gone lame. The children are in
the wagon. I told them to stay under the hay and blankets. If
I can get word to Doug, he'll be able to help." For once, he
didn't seem reluctant to talk.

The idea came to her from nowhere. "I'm sure Mr.
Danielson wouldn't mind if I took the children home with
me. That way you can do what needs to be done for your
horse without worrying about them alone at the farm or here
getting chilled."

"I really hate to put you out."

"It's not putting me out in the slightest. I'm glad for an
excuse to have your children with me. Come on, Phillip. How
would you, Greg, and Ruth like to spend the night at my
house?"

Timothy reached over the side of the wagon and helped his
daughter down first, then his sons. Ida thought he looked at
her strangely, but in the dark she couldn't be sure. Greg had
already started shivering, so she tucked him inside her cape.

"Ken, we need to hurry and get these children warm."

Phillip and Ruth clambered into the rumble seat. Ida kept Greg cuddled in front with her. Ken's silence told her loudly how much he resented her changing his plans. Couldn't he see the children needed help? To give him credit, however, he didn't dawdle getting them back to the boardinghouse.

Thankfully, Lucy had already arrived home. As soon as she saw the children, she bustled upstairs, returning with an armload of clothing that she laid out on chairs pulled near the stove. "I'm glad I've kept some of the grandchildren's clothes here. Ida, how about a warm bath for Phillip and Greg while I make up some beds? Ruth, I'll tuck you here next to the stove with a hot cup of tea, so you can get warm while we tend your brothers."

By the time Ida had finished bathing the boys, their pajamas had warmed through. She folded a blanket around each. "Mrs. Barry has two lovely beds upstairs. Would you rather sleep there or in my room?"

"With you," Phillip murmured sleepily.

Ruth caught Ida's attention and beckoned. "They can't sleep in the same bed," she whispered. "Phillip thrashes so much he keeps Greggy awake. I can take Greggy upstairs with me."

"In this house, you're a lady of leisure." Ida shook her head, feeling a tingly sense of delight at being able to remove a little of the burden from this girl's shoulders, even for a night. "Greggy can sleep with me." Phillip fell asleep almost before his head reached the pillow as Ida folded the blankets around him on his floor pallet beside her bed. Greg had drifted off while sitting in the kitchen. She gently moved him to her bed, making sure the covers were pulled snugly around his shoulders.

Ruth could barely keep her eyes open, but she wanted to

talk. "Miss Thomas, have you noticed my dad is different?"

"I don't know your dad that well." She had suspected change, but how could she admit to watching him?

"Well, he is. He noticed I wasn't so mad all the time, and asked me why. I told him about what you said, and what happened after that." She blushed, still embarrassed over her outburst. "That's when he said he'd start coming with me on Sundays. Mr. Pierce has been asking him for a long time, but he wouldn't do it until now."

Ida's curiosity had been piqued. "Does Mr. Pierce visit your dad a lot?"

"Not visit, exactly. He's just there whenever my dad needs help. He says he comes because he likes my cooking, but I think he just says that so Dad won't feel beholden. Sometimes Theo comes, too." Ruth yawned widely. "What I wanted to say is, I think God's answering our prayers for Dad."

Lucy entered the kitchen in time to catch Ruth's yawn. "If you'd like a bath, there's still lots of hot water. Unless you'd rather just go straight to bed."

"I am sleepy, but a real bath sounds heavenly. I usually just take sponge baths at home. Can I just sit in it for awhile?"

Ida swallowed the instinctive urge to correct Ruth's grammar. "Sit as long as you like."

Once Ruth's bathtub had been hauled to her room and filled, Ida and Lucy returned to the kitchen for chamomile tea and private conversation. "What brought this on?" Lucy wanted to know.

Ida explained about seeing the family by the side of the road, then remembered something. "I never did notice Ken leaving. He's probably feeling extremely put out with me."

Lucy watched her closely. "Would you have done anything differently to make him happier?"

"And leave those children out in the cold? Of course not." She felt miffed that Lucy could even ask.

Lucy grinned mysteriously. "Just checking. It's not every guy in town who can bring you flowers, candy, and a car, not to mention offering you a custom-built house with servants."

Ida swirled the tea in the bottom of her cup, thinking about her conversation with Ken as they drove. "I discovered something tonight. His gifts matter more to Ken than people do. The way he talked tonight, I felt almost like I'd been bribed." She chuckled. "He told me tonight I'm the perfect woman."

Lucy snickered. "Perfect for what?"

"I didn't ask. Somehow I didn't feel complimented."

"He wants to offer you anything money can buy, Ida."

"I know. But there's still something missing. I don't know what it is. If I did, I'd feel less like a shrew for not appreciating him."

Lucy put her hands over Ida's in the familiar gesture. "Honey, the book of Psalms tells us that if we delight in Him, God will give us the desires of our hearts. I think He's referring to the want itself as well as the satisfaction of the want. If He hasn't given you a desire for Ken's friendship, then cooperate with Him. He knows your heart and his. He has something planned for each of you that's better than either of you can imagine. Ken may be so self-centered he misses it. But I don't think you will."

"Thanks for the confidence." Footsteps upstairs indicated Ruth had finished her bath. "I'll help you dump the tub, and then I'm going to bed. This day has been almost too much."

Despite the unfamiliarity of another body in her bed, Ida slept dreamlessly. She awoke Sunday morning to find Greg had snuggled himself against her with his arms wrapped around one of hers. Cuddling with him felt so right, so . . . maternal.

Both boys seemed to wake simultaneously, Greg slowly stretching, Phillip talking immediately. "I forgot I was sleeping at your house, Miss Thomas. Do we have to go home today?"

She thought his choice of words amusing. "It depends on when your Daddy comes for you. Maybe you'll get to go to church with Mrs. Barry and me."

Breakfast was a noisy affair. Greg had awakened to full voice by that time, and Phillip hadn't slowed a bit. Ida expected Mr. Carey to make some grouchy comments. Instead, he listened to the chatter with a half-smile on his face and even helped Greg cut his pancakes. The women pretended not to notice. Lucy found some more clothes of her grandchildren's that sort of fit the boys. With a bit of tucking and basting, Ida's green and yellow plaid skirt fit Ruth, topped by a green sweater Lucy'd also found. All five of them bundled into the buggy to head for the "meeting house" at Spencers' farm. Mr. Carey once again declined Lucy's offer to accompany them, though she'd assured him the boys would love to have him along.

"I can tell I'm getting to him," she told Ida gleefully, expertly guiding the horse out of town. "He turned me down politely. It won't be long now before he lets God take over."

Despite Phillip's earlier eagerness to remain with Ida, he launched himself from the buggy as soon as he saw his dad, who'd just arrived with the Pierces. Ida couldn't hear what he was saying, but he obviously had plenty to tell Timothy. Surprisingly, Greg didn't seem to want to let her go. He insisted on sitting on her lap during the service, while Ruth sat on one side and Phillip snuggled closely on the other. Timothy settled a little awkwardly beside Phillip. Afterwards, Greg wanted Ida to fix his plate for him, which she managed to do while listening to Phillip describe his dream to her. When she caught Timothy watching, she smiled quickly before Greg directed her attention elsewhere.

Not until dishes had been cleaned up did Timothy finally speak to her. "Doug has loaned me one of his horses until Blackie's foot is better, so I can take the children home this afternoon."

"Would you like me to bring their clothes on Monday to save you the trip into town?" Greg was clamoring for another hug, so she picked him up.

Refusal had showed in his eyes until Greg hugged her. "I would appreciate that, ma'am."

Greg leaned over for a hug from his dad, so Timothy took him. Ida smiled at them, then turned to accompany Lucy out the door.

"Miss Thomas?"

She looked back at Timothy's uncertain expression.

"Thanks for. . .well, just thanks for everything."

ten

With the Christmas concert only ten days away, Ida used most afternoons for rehearsals. Patricia would play the part of Mary, and Young Lionel would be Joseph. Nettie, Michael, and June were the Three Wise Ones. They couldn't be Wise Men "'cause Nettie and June are *girls*," Phillip had pointed out with all the disdain small boys have for females not mature enough to be called women. David and four of the six-year-olds made credible shepherds. Tommy was the Star in the East, and Clara and Ruth formed a lop-sided pair of angels. Clara wanted to do the talking, though she couldn't seem to remember her first line, "Glory to God in the highest." Ruth showed amazing patience, reviewing the words over and over with the small actress. The older boys preferred to work on scenery and props, though Ida had persuaded Justin, Jed, and Theodore to do a short choral reading. She wanted to include Jim, as well, but he missed most practices.

"Had you thought about having some singing?" Cynthia asked, the Monday after the tobogganing party.

Ida had wished many times she could. "I'd love to, but I haven't figured out how to teach them without a piano. I don't sing well."

"Why don't you bring them over to our place? We have a piano, and I'd enjoy playing for them. I'm sure Doug wouldn't mind us using the team and wagon to get them back and forth."

Ida couldn't help contrasting the Pierces' generous sharing of their financial security with Ken's selfish squandering, then rebuked herself. *Don't be too hard on him. Maybe he hasn't been taught any differently.* But the feeling wouldn't go away.

The students reveled in the music practice sessions. Even the older boys, from whom she'd expected opposition, joined in the singing. Most of the children happily, though not always accurately, carried the melody. Justin was developing a marvelous bass voice, and Theodore had obviously already learned how to use his tenor. Ruth picked up alto harmony almost instinctively, and Patricia followed along well. Nettie's strong voice didn't surprise Ida, but its sweetness did. Her little choir would do her proud the week before Christmas.

Friday afternoon, Nina and Kate delivered the costumes. Ida couldn't imagine where they'd found the ideas. Creativity had transformed hand-me-downs into garments fit for stage, complete with sparkling jewelry for the Wise Ones and perfectly sized staves for the shepherds. Teddy and Phillip started a jousting match with theirs, so Ida declared the staves off limits until the dress rehearsal. She had a hunch Teddy would steal the show with his star costume, a huge six-pointed piece of cardboard with something sparkling stretched over it. His arms fit through straps on the back, and his cherubic face peeked through a hole near the center.

"You ladies are marvelous!" she exclaimed when the last piece had been revealed. "How did you think of so many great ideas?"

"Raising children develops a woman's creativity." Nina laughed, reaching for little Tabitha, who balanced precariously on top of a desk.

"In that case, you should be close to a genius," Kate remarked drily. "I've been thinking you must be trying to beat Ruby's record. I still can't figure out why anyone would want that many children. Of course, if all kids were as well-behaved as yours, it would make a difference. My two youngest can drive me insane without half trying." She seemed oblivious to both standing well within earshot.

Michael chose that moment to pull Nettie's hair, launching a scuffle which demanded Ida's immediate attention, and the two mothers left.

By Friday, Ida felt frazzled. Christmas excitement had invaded her classroom. While Justin, Theodore, and Ruth managed to maintain their studies, the rest of the students were far too wound up to concentrate. She tried to start the day with the customary arithmetic drill. Only David made any pretense of working, and over half his answers were incorrect. Next, she tried a spelling bee, but the six-year-olds couldn't participate and distracted everyone. All at once she remembered a box of colored paper Cynthia had given her. "Who wants to make Christmas cards?" She distributed the colored paper, glue, and scissors, thereby exchanging pandemonium for organized confusion. The project only required her mediation skills for settling debates as to who got to use which piece of paper and whose card looked prettiest. By the time the cards were finished and the classroom restored to tidiness, she could justify calling lunch. She allowed twenty minutes for eating, then shooed everyone outside. Hopefully, fifteen to thirty minutes of solitude would restore her supply of patience. The older children would have to settle any schoolyard debates. She was going to pretend she couldn't hear a thing. Folding her arms on her desk, she let her head fall forward.

"Miss Thomas?"

The whisper roused her from the brink of sleep to see Ruth standing beside her. Her smile came easily. "What can I do for you?"

Ruth extended a piece of paper. "I was wondering if I could read this poem at the concert."

Ida read. "It's beautiful, Ruth. Where did you find it?"

She studied Ida's desktop self-consciously. "It was just in my head."

"You mean you wrote it? I didn't know you were a poet."

"I'm not, really." The girl beamed, albeit shyly. "I just wanted to read it because it tells what I feel about Christmas this year. You won't tell anyone I wrote it, will you?"

"Of course I won't, if that's what you want. But why not?"

"I don't want them to laugh at me." She shrugged and wrinkled her nose.

Ida could understand. Reading the verses as part of a planned program was one thing. Admitting to having written them would be opening her soul for observation, not all of it gentle or kind. "I won't tell."

Afternoon practice didn't go much better than morning classes. No one remembered their lines correctly, the shepherds refused to stand still, and even the choral readers couldn't seem to get their timing correct. At two o'clock, she gave up and sent everyone home. "Theodore, will you please tell your mother we won't be coming?" She thought she saw understanding in his smile as he nodded, but he didn't say anything.

As soon as the last child had bundled up and disappeared down the road, Ida saddled Misty. If she stayed around to clean up, this would be one of the days Ken would show up to accompany her home. This way, he'd only find an empty schoolhouse.

"The day must have been brutal," Lucy observed when she arrived home. "It's early, and you look like you were pulled through a knothole backwards."

Ida chuckled, feeling some of the day's tension drain away. "I'm almost ready to outlaw Christmas. Even Patricia, who rarely says an unkind word to anyone, told Matthew he was a stupid donkey for stepping on the edge of her costume. Karin burst into tears because David made a face at her, and Nettie spent the day telling me how I should do things differently. Justin, Theo, and Ruth were the only ones who achieved anything remotely resembling studying."

"Just one day like that won't hurt any of them," Lucy soothed, pouring her a cup of peppermint tea. "You did right sending them home early. Let their parents cope with that excess energy. Why don't you take a rest and I'll wake you in plenty of time to freshen up for supper."

Ida could feel her eyelids drooping at the mere suggestion. "You're sure you don't need help with supper?"

"I'll call when you're needed." Lucy smiled mysteriously.

Dusk had already darkened her window when Lucy's gentle tap brought her awake. Her disorientation lasted only until she heard, "You've just enough time to freshen up, dear."

Time? Ida checked the wall clock, remembering Lucy's strange expression earlier. Just past five. What was her friend up to? She'd just barely finished pinning her hair up again when she detected a ruckus in the front entry.

"I'm here, Miss Thomas. Are you s'prised?" As soon as Ida came out of her room, Phillip launched himself into her welcoming arms. "Mrs. Barry asked us to come for supper and not to tell you 'cause it was s'posed to be a s'prise. I didn't say anything at school today or yesterday or the day before, did I? Are you s'prised?"

"Slow down, son," Timothy advised, putting a large hand on Phillip's head as he passed.

"Yes, I'm surprised," Ida assured the excited boy, helping Greg climb into her lap, too. "And how are you, Mr. Greg?"

"I'm just Greg," he informed her solemnly. "Know what I did today?"

"No. What?" Ida looked up briefly to give Ruth a

welcoming smile.

"We builded a fire at school."

Ida was sure she hadn't heard correctly. "You what?" The blush creeping out from the edges of Timothy's beard indicated maybe the story wasn't so farfetched.

"Daddy goes to school every morning before it gets light outside, 'cause he says he has to make it warm." Phillip started the story, but Greg took over quickly, his head bobbing emphatically. "I woked up before he left, and Ruthie was busy, so Dad tooked me with him. I helpted him, didn't I, Dad?" He looked at his red-faced father for confirmation.

"You did, son."

Somehow this piece of knowledge created a funny feeling in Ida's middle. She tried to ignore her reaction and ease Timothy's embarrassment. "You must have done a good job, Greg, because the school was just toasty when I got there. I've really appreciated that fire every single morning, but I had no idea you and your dad made it." Her gaze met Timothy's over the boys' heads. For the first time, his contained something other than heart-rending grief, something almost personal. A warm tingle spread along her spine. Where did she get the feeling his early morning trips to the schoolhouse were a personal gesture? Impossible. He still mourned his wife intensely. She shifted her eyes guiltily as she realized the direction of her thoughts, only to find Lucy watching.

Lucy's gaze dropped to the children. "Boys, how about giving Miss Thomas some room to breathe? If you'll go upstairs to the room with the door open, you'll find some toys. Ruth, would you set the table for me?"

Ida turned abruptly to show Ruth where to find plates and eating utensils. The boys returned, each with a wooden truck that they rushed to show their dad. Timothy gave each son several moments of individual attention, then addressed them both. "Just make sure you don't get in the ladies' way, boys, and be ready to come as soon as Mrs. Barry calls us."

"Yes, sir," they chorused. Loud simulations of truck noises soon emerged from the hallway.

Ida kept herself busy mashing potatoes and putting fresh rolls into a towel-lined bowl. It didn't help. Timothy's presence created a tingle of awareness she couldn't escape. She found herself smiling at his gentle conversation with his sons, impressed with the way he gave each individual attention. *Doug Pierce and Lionel Spencer treated their children similarly. Why should Timothy seem so remarkable?* She took care to avoid eye contact with him during supper, not an easy feat since Lucy had placed them across the table from each other. A knock at the door during dessert offered her escape. "I'll get it, Lucy."

Ken Danielson stood on the step, holding a carefully wrapped package. "Hi! May I come in?"

Ida stepped aside wordlessly. The familiar light scent of his aftershave almost caused her to cringe. His gift held no appeal, either. His hands caught her attention—white, carefully groomed, no dirt ground into the pores, no rough callouses.

"Is this a bad time?" he asked softly, as if trying to keep the conversation private from those seated at the table behind Ida.

She lifted her gaze to the cultured lines of his face, forcing a smile on her own. "No. Lucy just has guests for supper, but you'd be welcome to share pie with us."

"I'd rather just be with you. Would you mind going for a walk?"

For some reason she couldn't identify, she minded very much. "I've had a difficult day at school. I'd rather stay inside. I hope that's okay."

He caught at her hand, a frown creasing his forehead. "I was hoping we could really talk tonight."

"About what?" She pulled back, wishing he'd quit trying to be so personal. Whispers and footsteps behind her indicated Lucy had shepherded everyone into the sitting room.

"I asked you awhile ago if I could come courting. You've never said yes or no." Rather than uncertainty, his eyes revealed only displeasure.

A mental picture suddenly intruded into her dilemma—a tall, skinny man kneeling in front of the schoolhouse stove, hurrying to get wood burning so he could leave without being seen, then his blush when his son revealed his activities; a broken-hearted gaze warming ever so slightly. The scarred soul she'd glimpsed held far more appeal than the polished creature who now waited for her answer. She would probably never see more of the inner Timothy McEvan. What she had seen convinced her she couldn't be satisfied with Ken's luxuries. She craved character more than culture, depth more than polish.

"Ida?"

"I'm sorry." She directed a half-hearted smile at him. "I've just been thinking."

"And your answer?" He squeezed her hand so hard it hurt.

"It wouldn't work."

He let go abruptly. Disbelief twisted his expression. "But . . . but . . . but why? You would make a beautiful wife. You'd never have to teach again, and would never have to do without anything."

She touched his arm to stop the flow of words. "I'm sorry, Mr. Danielson. I've enjoyed your company, but I don't feel toward you as a woman should toward any man she permits to court her."

"That doesn't matter." His voice grew louder with fervency. "I care enough for both of us."

His selfishness eliminated her fear of hurting him. "The answer is simply and finally no. I think you should just go now." She was hardly aware she was whispering fiercely in reaction to his loud protest while she thrust the unopened package into his hands. "Good night, Mr. Danielson."

He said nothing more as he left, his expression sullen. Ida stood in the open doorway, momentarily oblivious to the biting cold which swirled around her. She'd just refused what probably represented her only opportunity for marriage in this tiny community. But she couldn't feel regret. Despite his age and size, Ken remained little more than a boy. Somewhere, somehow, she hoped to meet a man. Someone who had matured inside as well as outside. Someone with whom she could share her soul with all its scars and bruises and who would share his in return.

"Are you all right, Ida?"

Lucy's voice from behind returned her to reality. She nodded reassuringly as she shut the door. "Sorry about the draft. It was Mr. Danielson."

"He didn't stay long."

"He saw we had company." She mentally reached for a smile which would mask the turmoil into which her emotions had been stirred.

The rest of the evening passed pleasantly enough. Mr. Carey and Timothy discussed crops, weather, and animals—those subjects of perennial interest to farmers. Ruth and Lucy visited cheerily over dishpans. Greg and Phillip took turns telling Ida long-winded stories.

After a final cup of coffee, Timothy bundled his family up for the ride home. "Thanks for the dinner, Mrs. Barry."

Lucy beamed at him. "You'll have to come more often."

Ida accepted a round of hugs from the children, wondering at the gleam in her friend's eyes. And why did the room seem so empty when the McEvanses departed?

eleven

The five school days prior to the Christmas concert left Ida little time to feel Ken's absence. She insisted on diligent study in the mornings that required as much effort from her as from the students. Friday right after lunch, Doug Pierce arrived with a wagon filled with hay to take the excited group into town for "dress rehearsal" in the makeshift performance hall. Ida gasped with delighted surprise at the changes Lionel and Lars had created in what had been a dingy storage room.

A sturdy square wooden platform stood at one end. Temporary curtains basted from Nina's linen supply hid all but the center area from spectator view, providing "backstage" changing and waiting areas. The men had scrounged enough benches from somewhere to provide seating for a sizable crowd. She wondered if more than the first few rows would be filled.

The different environment increased the students' already fever-pitch excitement. Clara forgot her opening line again and burst into tears. Nettie suddenly announced she was "tired of this stupid play." Ruth moved to comfort Clara while Ida tried to find the reason for Nettie's temper. Meanwhile, the shepherds got into another squabble, which resulted in a broken staff. More tears.

Just when Ida felt she'd burst into tears herself, Doug stepped in. "Students, let's give Miss Thomas a break for a moment. Come sit down here." He waved toward the benches.

Hearing his quiet authority, even Nettie cooperated. No one fidgeted as he continued to speak in gentle tones. "You

110

students have done a wonderful job preparing for this concert. You'll be a real credit to Miss Thomas, and your parents will be proud of you. But can anyone tell me why you're doing this?"

"'Cause it's fun?" Michael piped up.

"I suppose that's part of it," Doug affirmed, glancing apologetically at Ida, who presently felt like the project was anything but fun. "There's more to it than that, though. Why are you singing the kinds of songs you are, and doing the play you're doing? Why not some other story?"

They thought for several moments, then Justin raised his hand. "It is Christmas time, sir, so that's our theme."

"And what's so special about Christmas?"

"That's when Jesus was borned," Sara answered promptly.

"So you're really doing this program because of Jesus, right?" Doug raised his eyebrows in question. When several nodded enthusiastically, he inquired, "Do you think maybe Jesus wants to help us all remember our lines, listen to Miss Thomas, and get along with each other?"

Ida noticed Nettie's softened expression. Somehow she hadn't credited the girl with enough heart to care about spiritual matters. Mentally asking divine forgiveness for overlooking the positive in one of her most troublesome students, she heard Doug ask the children to bow their heads.

"Let's pray right now, and ask Jesus to help us all tell His story the best we can. Lord Jesus, we're all here today because we want to celebrate Your birth by telling others how You came. We've never tried anything like this before, and we're all a little jittery about it. Would You please help each one of us to remember what we're supposed to do and say, and give us willing spirits to get along with one another? Please bless Miss Thomas for working with us so patiently. We want others to find out how wonderful You are through what we do here tonight. Thank you. In Jesus' name, Amen."

Everyone calmed down miraculously after that. Even the youngest children seemed to have taken Doug's words to heart. By the time the wagon full of students left shortly after three, Ida felt relatively confident the evening would be a success.

The house was still when she entered. *Lucy must be resting*, Ida thought as she eased her bedroom door open so it wouldn't squeak, then stopped abruptly. A gorgeous dress hung from a hook on the wall. Made from a deliciously rich shade of red satiny fabric, it had long puffy sleeves fastened with tiny pearl buttons on each long lace-edged cuff. A high collar rimmed with lace topped a form-fitting bodice. Yards of the shiny material hung in long, graceful folds from an impossibly small waistline. She felt Lucy's presence behind her even before she spoke.

"Well, what do you think?"

Ida turned to her friend. "It's lovely. Where did it come from?"

Lucy's excitement gentled into compassion. "I thought you might be missing your mother's fine needlework for Christmas, and decided to try to fill the gap."

Tears stung. Ida hadn't been aware until now how hard she'd been trying not to think about past holidays. Lucy's embrace softened the loneliness. Her beautiful gift made Ida realize how much she'd gained since last Christmas even though she'd also lost much. "Thank you, Lucy." She pulled back and wiped her eyes. "It looks too small, though."

"Only because you're used to wearing clothes almost too big for you," Lucy replied briskly. "Try it on. I'll bet it fits perfectly."

It did, too. Despite the unaccustomed snug fit, Ida felt gorgeous rather than indecent. "How did you figure out my size?"

Lucy laughed. "I just borrowed a couple of dresses while

you were at school, then adjusted the measurements for the different pattern. I've had a hunch a lovely figure hid behind your baggy clothes."

Ida felt a twinge of discomfort, which she didn't know how to explain without hurting Lucy's generous heart.

But Lucy guessed what she was thinking, and her voice softened. "It's not sin to be pretty, you know."

"Mom always said beauty was dangerous, that it could get me into trouble."

"If you flaunt it, yes. Any of God's gifts can be dangerous if used contrary to His purposes." Lucy reached for both of Ida's hands. "But, my dear girl, your gentle, pure spirit shines out through those lovely green eyes so brightly, no one could ever accuse you of misusing His gift of beauty."

Ida raised her gaze to Lucy's eyes. "A gift? I've always thought of it as a temptation, pride for me, and wrong thoughts for men."

"It's the way God made you, isn't it?"

Ida nodded.

"Then it's His gift to you." She paused. "And to the man He'll bring as your husband."

Ida could feel warmth spreading up her neck, but she had to pursue the subject. "What do you mean?"

"God has made men to be attracted by physical beauty. That's why flaunted prettiness does tempt men to impure thoughts. You've learned to keep your appearance disciplined by discretion, and I think God will use it as a special joy for someone who needs an extra daily reminder of how good He is. Now, why don't you let me set up a nice, hot bath for you down here. Soak as long as you want, and I'll bring supper in when you're finished so you can eat in your dressing gown. That way you can rest and spend as much time as you need prettying up."

Ida pondered Lucy's words while she reveled in the warm, scented water. The tub was just large enough so she could sit with her legs bent comfortably. She chuckled to herself. If she were any taller, she would have been cramped. As a teenager, she'd often wished she were at least three inches taller and quite a bit plainer. Mom's warnings about her appearance had made her feel like an invitation to trouble. *Had Mom been overzealous?* It felt horribly disloyal to be questioning her views when she couldn't explain herself. Another of Mom's quotes came to mind. "Think for yourself, girl. That's why God gave you a mind that works." Of course, that statement had always been used to answer Ida's questions about views she heard in her classes which were different from the way she'd always thought. Ida looked again at the crimson gown. Mom would have thought the color too attention-getting, as well. But Lucy loved God as much as Mom had. She wouldn't have given Ida the dress if she felt it were sinful, either in color or style. Maybe Mom's perspective on Ida's appearance was simply personal preference, rather than divine guidance. Ida decided to wear it to the concert and watch people's reactions. If it elicited any kind of attention that she felt was improper, she'd simply explain the problem to Lucy and not wear it again.

But once Ida arrived at the scene of the night's entertainment, all thoughts of personal appearance fled. One of the curtains needed a quick fix. Students began arriving, dressed in their best, some already exhibiting signs of stage fright. Theo, in black trousers and a white shirt, handed over the repaired shepherd's staff, while Ruth looked at her with wide green eyes. "Miss Thomas, are you sure my poem's good enough to read out loud?"

Ida took time to hug her. "Do you think I'd let you do something which would embarrass you?"

Ruth pulled back and looked into Ida's face for several moments, then down at the floor. "I guess not."

Ida gently pulled on the girl's chin until her head lifted again. "I love you, Ruth, and your poem is just right. What you've written may be exactly what someone needs to hear tonight."

Ruth pulled in a deep gulp of air. "I'm just scared they'd laugh if they knew I wrote it."

"No one will laugh, I promise." Ida smiled reassuringly. "You look lovely."

Ruth pulled self-consciously at her deep green skirt with its ruffled flounce. A lace-trimmed cream blouse brought out the deep highlights in her wavy red hair, which she'd tied into a simple low ponytail with a bow matching her skirt. "Mrs. Pierce made it for me for the concert. You look really nice, too, Miss Thomas."

"Thank you, Ruth." She silently lifted a prayer of thanksgiving. She'd noticed how drab Ruth's few dresses had become. *Bless Cynthia for doing something about it for this evening.* Maybe Nina would make a couple more if Ida bought the fabric. She glanced quickly around the rapidly filling room, but to her relief, Ken hadn't come. For just a moment, her gaze intercepted Timothy's. Something she saw made her conscious once again of her appearance. She turned quickly back to her students.

The play went off without a hitch. Clara remembered her lines, the shepherds behaved themselves, and no one tripped over anyone else's clothing. Both the choral reading and the group singing with two-part harmony brought enthusiastic applause. Ruth's poem was the last item of the evening. The packed room fell silent as the girl knelt beside the makeshift manger and began to speak in a quiet, yet resonant voice.

"They say he's just a baby,

And in part they're right.
He cries, drinks only milk,
And awakens through the night.
It seems almost unreal
This mewling infant could be more
Yet Scripture had foretold
His coming here so long before.
His Father called Him Mighty God,
Wonderful, Prince of Peace.
He offers life eternal
Amazing love that will not cease.
Many years have passed.
Happily we celebrate His birth.
But what He does for me each day
Is of much more worth.
My life had turned bleak shades of gray
Then windy storms turned clouds black.
But then I saw Him standing there.
His smile rolled storm clouds back.
No matter where I am,
I know He's on my side.
Within His healing love,
I'm learning to abide.
He is my Prince of Peace."

Ida knew the audience's knowledge of Ruth's family added meaning to the simple words. Sure enough, she could hear light sniffs and quiet blowing of noses as Ruth disappeared behind the curtain. Under Ida's direction, the audience sang "Silent Night" in closing. Before the carol ended, Lionel Spencer had joined Ida at the front of the room, and indicated he wanted to speak.

He cleared his throat when the last musical notes faded.

"Well, folks, I'm not much of a public speaker, but someone had to say these words. We thought the superintendent of our school board ought to do it, but Lars declined." Everyone chuckled at the idea of the silent Lars Harper addressing a crowd. "First, we want to thank you townfolk who graciously came to see our children's program tonight. We'd like to give credit to the special lady who made it possible. Miss Ida Thomas came to us from Edmonton in September to teach in our country school. As you witnessed tonight, she's done a wonderful job. Miss Thomas, in thanks from all the parents of your students, please accept this gift."

Ida couldn't blink fast enough to keep the tears back as the entire audience stood and clapped enthusiastically. She could feel the love these usually reticent people were trying to express in their applause. Lionel motioned for her to open the brightly wrapped package. She untied the red yarn bow, then folded back green paper. Inside lay a pair of navy blue woolen mittens trimmed in pink nestled on top of a pink scarf with navy tassels and a navy-trimmed pink hat. "I don't know what to say." Her voice wouldn't come out loud enough. "Thanks for the gift, and thanks for the privilege of working with your children."

Another round of applause broke out, then the crowd began filing to the tables at the side of the room where the ladies had placed a mouth-watering array of baked goodies. Ida turned toward the platform, where her students waited as a group.

"We did it, Miss Thomas." Young Lionel beamed.

Clara's eyes sparkled. "And I didn't forget my words."

"You all did very well." Ida gave each student a touch on the shoulder, hand, or head to let them know how proud she felt. "I want you all to have a wonderful two weeks off and be prepared to study hard when you come back."

There were a few groans at the suggestion, but everyone was smiling. The younger children started the round of hugs, which ended up including every student, except the three older boys who confined themselves to manly handshakes.

When the last one vanished in the direction of the goodies, Ida turned to find Nina waiting to speak with her. "I just wanted to tell you how beautiful you look tonight, Ida. That color suits you wonderfully. Is that dress another of your mother's creations?"

Again Ida had to choke back tears. "No. Lucy made it for me."

Nina gathered her into a hug. "This time of year can't be easy being in a totally new place with people you hadn't met until four months ago. I hope it helps to know how much we've come to love you."

"Thanks." Ida wiped her wet cheeks.

Nina smiled understandingly, then moved through the crowd toward her husband.

Ida watched, feeling an unfamiliar twist of envy. Everyone here had someone. Her gaze found Doug and Cynthia talking to a couple from town, Doug's arm draped around Cynthia's shoulders. She made her way to the door. Maybe some time outside looking at the stars and breathing the sharp, cold air would restore her perspective. Her cape lay near the bottom of the pile of wraps beside the door. She found it and wrapped it around herself, feeling more desolate than ever. If only Mom were here to share this evening with her. If only she could feel Mom's arms around her, rather than this lifeless reminder of her absence. Moving into the shadows beside the door, she leaned against the building, willing herself not to break down completely. She began to whisper into the cold night air. "Mom, I don't know if you can hear me, but I need to talk to you. You don't know any of these people, so I can't even imagine that you're rejoicing at what we accomplished tonight. Even the dress I'm wearing isn't something you would have made for me, probably isn't even a dress you'd like. I'm changing, Mom, and I feel like I'm losing you in the process."

Changes. Ida pondered all that had happened since she'd come to Dawson Creek. She felt like she was becoming part of this remote community. Not so remote anymore, she reminded herself. The first train ever was due to arrive sometime in the new year and would provide weekly service. Maybe Ken would be able to find a bride in the city and bring her back on the train. The thought of him marrying someone else brought relief. At least she'd know she hadn't hurt him irreparably. But would she ever find her kind of mate?

A sound beyond the edge of the building caught her attention. She listened for a moment longer. There it was again. A heart-wrenching sob broke from the shadows. Cautiously, she stepped away from her hiding place and moved toward the sound. Gradually, she could make out a form against the neighboring feed store. She couldn't be sure, but she thought she recognized the long, skinny outline.

"Mr. McEvan?" she called softly. When no response came, she paused. She really had no right to intrude, but his and his children's agony had almost become her own. Yet another change on her inner landscape since— Another sob interrupted her thoughts. A compulsion moved her close enough to confirm her conclusion. "Timothy, it's me, Ida." The shadow against the wall seemed to change posture slightly. *Had he heard her?* "I only heard you because I've been out here grieving, too. Somehow Christmas makes death so much harder to bear." She paused to see if he would respond. She had almost decided to leave him alone when muffled words stopped her.

"It's just not fair."

How well she knew that feeling! Somehow she had to keep him talking. "What do you mean?"

Through the darkness, she could barely see him turn to face her. "Janet should have been here to hear Ruthie tonight. Daniel would have been so proud of his sister, and of Phillip. And Sam and Benjamin. They all would have been here if I hadn't failed them."

Ida felt like his anger had grabbed her around the middle. She forced her voice not to tremble. "How is it your fault, Timothy?"

"I should have taken the rafts over myself one at a time. I should have waited until winter so we could have crossed on ice. I don't really know what I should have done. If I'd just done something different, I wouldn't have lost them." Another sob broke from him.

She prayed for the right ideas, the right words. Was there any way she could pull this man back from the precipice of guilt and heartbreak? "I never knew your wife, Timothy, but Ruth has told me a bit about her, and a bit more about Daniel. I don't think either one of them would want you to beat yourself up over what happened. I know you miss them. I still miss my dad and he's been gone thirteen years."

He replied brokenly, "But my wife. My boys. I'm supposed to protect them. I failed."

She moved close enough to lay her hands on his arms. "You're not God. You couldn't have saved your family from the river any more than I could have saved my mother from tuberculosis. It's hard to go on without them, but we have to. Both of us do."

"How?" The single syllable was cut off by another sob.

"I don't know exactly. I just take one day at a time. When the hurt starts to overwhelm me, I remind myself that God understands what I can't. I don't have to explain what He allows, only trust Him to help me bear it."

He shook her hands off his arms and moved a couple of steps away. "I used to love God. How can I now? That hurts as much as anything. Now when I need Him so much, I can't feel anything toward Him except anger for what He's taken away." His voice dropped to a ragged whisper. "Sometimes I even hate Him."

Another plea for divine help launched itself from Ida's heart. She stepped close enough to touch him again. "He knows. Scripture tells us He's felt everything we feel, and that He captures each of our tears and keeps them in a bottle. If He cares enough to collect our tears, I think He understands our anger."

"But will it ever end?" He bowed his head onto her shoulder. Her cape absorbed his tears.

Awkwardly, she wrapped her arms around his heaving shoulders. Some might think her actions improper, but God knew her heart. Maybe for the moment, He saw them only as two human beings clinging to each other in their search for Him. She had no idea where the thought came from, but it gave her courage to speak as she tightened her embrace. "I think the pain and anger only end when we stop trying to fight them. As long as we resist grieving, we only make the wounds worse. When we let ourselves hurt, we allow His healing to touch us."

Gradually, his weeping stilled. He straightened, then reached for her hand. "This is the first year my children have asked about Christmas since the river. I know it would help them, but I just can't do it."

The words came without conscious thought. "Why don't the four of you join Lucy and me at the boardinghouse on Christmas Day? You don't have to do anything except come."

He squeezed her hand, then let it go. "I'd better hitch up the team and get my family home."

Ida stayed outside awhile longer to give her emotions time to settle. For some reason, Timothy had bared his broken heart to her. In the uncharacteristic act of embracing him, she absorbed some of his hurt into her own bruised soul. Shared pain had formed a fragile bond between them.

twelve

At Lucy's insistence, Ida did nothing but rest the first four days of Christmas break. She slept until she felt like waking up, lounged around the house during the day, and went to bed early. By Wednesday morning, she felt more refreshed than she believed possible. "What can I do to help you get ready for company tomorrow?" she asked as she accepted a plate of pancakes for breakfast.

"Company," Mr. Carey snorted. "Good thing I'm leavin' for Hythe this afternoon, else I'd be trapped in this house with Merry Christmases and Scripture readings all day!"

Lucy's eyes twinkled. "You don't have to run off, Mr. Carey. We're having roast turkey and dressing, with mashed potatoes and the gravy you like so well, along with sweetened yams, boiled carrots, cranberry sauce which I made myself this summer, and three kinds of pie for dessert. I'm sure there will be plenty for you. We'll even warn you before we say 'Merry Christmas' so you can get out of earshot."

"Harrumph," was all he said as he left the table.

"Poor man," Lucy commented.

The phrase reminded Ida of Timothy huddled against the side of the feed store after the concert. *Would he and the children come tomorrow?* She'd heard no confirmation, but then he hadn't said they wouldn't come.

When she'd told Lucy about it, the older woman had smiled with a knowing twinkle in her eyes. "I'm glad you're feeling enough at home to invite people over. Let's plan on them being here. If they don't come, we'll just have extra food we can send home with Lionel and Nina."

Ida couldn't decide whether or not she wanted the McEvans to show up. Would she and Timothy even be comfortable in the same room after their intensely personal discussion? Yet if they didn't come, the rejection would feel equally personal. Just in case, she managed to find small gifts for each of the children: a red wooden truck for Greg, a blue one for Phillip, and a clothbound blank book Ruth could use for a diary or in which to write more poetry. Nina and Lucy had also managed to create two skirts and three blouses from fabrics the ladies had picked out together. Nina and Lucy had insisted on contributing to the cost. The parcel would be presented to Ruth from the three of them. She hadn't decided whether or not to find a gift for Timothy.

The family hadn't even attended the Sunday service at Spencers' farm. She had a feeling Timothy was still struggling with his feelings about God. For his sake, she hoped he could find peace. After that. . . She refused to let herself indulge in daydreams. At present, she felt strongly attracted to a widower who still felt married. Until he made peace with himself and his God, she'd best not let herself get carried away. But that didn't stop her from mentioning his name frequently in prayer.

She and Lucy scrubbed, swept, and baked all morning. By mid-afternoon, the house glowed with cleanliness and shimmered with delicious smells. After a light lunch, they lingered at the table over cups of tea.

"I think I'll take a bit of a rest," Lucy commented. "Lionel said he'd drop by around five with our tree. Thanks to you, everything else is ready. I'll make the dressing and stuff the turkey just before bedtime, so it can bake overnight. Is there anything you'd like to do, any way I can help make Christmas more like your mother used to?"

Ida smiled gratefully. Lucy's offer brought both pain and comfort. "This Christmas has already been more lavish than anything I can remember after Dad went off to war. We never had enough money to do anything but read the Christmas story and give each other a single, simple gift." She paused. "Our life together was often difficult, but I'd go back in a minute if it meant I'd still have Mom."

Lucy nodded. "I don't doubt you would, dear. Speaking of wealth and poverty, I haven't noticed Mr. Danielson around much."

"When he stopped by the other night while McEvanses were here, I told him I wasn't interested in being courted."

"What brought you to that conclusion? Or do you not want to talk about it?"

Ida looked into Lucy's compassion-filled eyes. If Mom had been here, she would have spilled out the whole story days ago. Maybe it was time to start letting go of Mom, and accept Lucy's mothering. "He's too much of a little boy who's used to getting his own way. He offered me every luxury he could think of, but he wouldn't take the time to discover the person I am inside."

"And?" Lucy seemed to be expecting a different kind of answer.

Ida studied her tea cup. "He's not the kind of man I could spend the rest of my life with."

"How did you discover that?"

Lucy's gentle inquiry compelled Ida to be honest. "Timothy McEvan."

A familiar glint shone in Lucy's eyes. "I suspected as much."

"There's a lot of strength and goodness buried in him. He's just hurting too badly to let it show."

"It seems to me a certain schoolteacher is luring it into the open."

Startled, Ida looked straight at Lucy. "What makes you say that? As near as I can tell, he still thinks of himself as married to Janet."

"Timothy used to keep himself strictly apart from his neighbors. I'm not sure what would have happened to him if Doug Pierce hadn't refused to be rejected. The only thing that surprised me more than seeing him at Sunday meeting was when he accepted my invitation to dinner. He studies you pretty carefully, you know."

"What do you mean?"

"Take the night of the concert, for instance. He watched you the entire evening, or at least until Ruth recited her poem."

"What happened then?"

"He just sort of seemed to crumble inside. As soon as Ruth joined him, he handed Greg to her and left. I didn't see him again."

"I did," Ida admitted softly.

"I noticed you going outside, but I thought you were just looking for a few moments to yourself."

"I was." Tears filled her eyes, remembering. "Everything around here is so different from what Mom and I lived. I feel like I've settled so securely into life here I'm losing touch with Mom."

"That's what healing's all about, honey." Lucy placed her hands over Ida's. "And I'm sure your Mom's glad to see it."

"I don't know." Ida shook her head. "I just had to get outside where I could talk to her without people thinking I'm going crazy. Somehow it helped."

"Sure it did. I still talk to both Kelvin and William from time to time, especially when my children or grandchildren make me proud. Those we've loved will always be part of our lives even though we have to live without them. That's why Timothy's going to need an exceptionally understanding wife if he decides to marry again." She refilled their teacups.

"He's a long way from that yet." Ida related what had happened by the feed store. She laughed self-consciously. "I'm glad no one could have seen us. They'd have been scandalized to see their proper schoolmarm embracing one of the parents who'd hired her." She searched for understanding in Lucy's gaze. "Maybe I am going a bit crazy, but I had the feeling God didn't see us so much as man and woman at that moment, but as two individuals seeking and giving comfort."

"It's not crazy at all, Ida. Scripture teaches that in Christ there is no Jew or Gentile, bond or free, male or female. Granted, here on earth, there's certainly a difference. But every once in a while, He gives us an opportunity to share His love in a way that goes past traditional barriers. Heart attitude is what makes the difference between that kind of ministry and simply disregarding His principles. You have a wonderfully generous heart. Don't be surprised if God is using it in unusual ways."

"Then I guess that's my excuse for inviting them all over here for Christmas."

"No need to apologize. In fact, I'm glad to see it. I have a hunch God has a very special place for you in Timothy McEvan's life. Had you thought about gifts for them?"

"I have something for each of the children, but I can't decide what, if anything, I should do for him."

Lucy thought for a moment. "I have an idea. I'll be right back."

Ida heard footsteps upstairs, then Lucy returned with something in her hand. "My William used to like to carve. He made a set of these for me less than a year before he died. I'd be pleased if you'd give this one to Timothy from you and me."

There certainly could be nothing improper about a gift from both of them. Ida studied the carving Lucy had placed on the table. It depicted an eagle with wings outstretched, each feather etched with meticulous detail, the wood polished to a glowing luster. "It's beautiful."

"William loved eagles. He used to read everything he could find about them. Did you know they seem to be able to sense when a storm is coming, and will fly directly into the wind until they're on top of the disturbance? He used to say that's the way he wanted to be as a Christian. But he also found out there are times when an eagle will wait out a storm. Rather than flying above it, he'll sit huddled on the ground or in a tree or up against a rock face. That was my favorite fact. Scripture says God will give us wings like eagles, but there are some times we just aren't able to fly above our heartaches. There's nothing wrong with waiting them out, as long as we don't stay huddled in our tree after the sun's come out."

Ida chuckled at Lucy's analogy. "That is a wonderful thought. I'll give this to him from both of us, and maybe some day I'll be able to tell him what you've told me."

❧

Christmas morning dawned bright and cold. Sunlight glinted off the snow in dazzling sparkles, yet the chill took her breath away when she went out to the stable to feed the horses. *Surely Timothy wouldn't bring his children out in this cold just for dinner.* She tried to push away disappointment.

Less than an hour later, the Spencers arrived, heralded by

bells Lionel had attached to his team's harness. Tabitha went immediately to the parlor, where the tree stood splashed with colorful fabric decorations. She squealed when she saw gifts piled around it.

"Not yet, Tabby," her mother admonished, adding two more packages to the collection. "We have to wait until Grandma tells us we can open them."

Tommy had to show Miss Thomas his new picture book "with words in it since I can read now," he declared proudly.

"And what do you have?" Ida asked Clara.

The shy little girl just tugged on the red scarf that hung around her neck even though her coat had been taken to the upstairs bedroom. David and Young Lionel joined the discussion, describing the puppies they'd received but had been unable to bring to Grandma's. In the middle of Young Lionel's description of his puppy, her concentration vanished. Had she heard arrivals at the front door?

A moment later, Phillip's familiar call confirmed her hopes. "Miss Thomas! I'm here."

She couldn't help the grin that plastered itself across her face. "I have to go greet our other guests," she informed the group around her. Even when she saw Timothy behind his children, she had trouble believing he had actually come. A quick glance at his eyes revealed the ghost of a smile.

Ruth reached out for a hug. "I can't believe we're here, Miss Thomas," she whispered. "Dad told me you'd invited us, but he didn't make up his mind until this morning. I thought he was going to decide it was too cold."

"Me too," Ida whispered back. She untied the boys' scarves, lifted woolen hats, tucked mittens into coat sleeves, and carried the pile of wraps to the designated bedroom upstairs. When she returned, Phillip and Greg were playing trucks with

Tommy, Ruth was helping Lucy and Nina in the kitchen, and Lionel had engaged Timothy in discussion while standing guard on the Christmas tree. While she added her assistance to meal preparation, she kept an ear tuned to the men's conversation. Though she couldn't distinguish words, she felt relieved to hear Timothy's rumbling tones regularly. She'd feel terrible if he didn't enjoy himself.

"Time to gather around the tree," Lucy announced after checking the turkey. "By the time we're finished, this bird should be ready to eat."

Lionel pulled an extra chair from the kitchen that he placed beside the armchair in which his wife sat. Lucy settled into the armchair closest to the tree, leaving only the small sofa for Timothy and Ida. Greg and Phillip eliminated any possible uneasiness over the seating arrangement by both trying to squeeze into the small space between their dad and Phillip's teacher. Ida pulled Greg into a hug at the same moment Timothy lifted Phillip onto his lap.

"We settled that pretty quickly, didn't we?" Timothy's eyes twinkled slightly with the humor Ida had known he possessed but had never seen. She simply nodded.

Lucy was speaking. "I'm thankful each of you were able to make it today. There's nothing quite like being able to share Christmas with those you love. Both Ida and the McEvan family have lost loved ones recently. Though there's no way a holiday can be the same as it was, we hope you'll find comfort and joy in the love of our family. Lionel." She turned to her son, who had a Bible spread on his lap.

He began reading the Christmas story. For the first time, Ida became aware that Mary and Joseph were separated from their loved ones on that "first Christmas." More importantly, that which made Christmas possible was Jesus' willingness to be separated from His Father, first in leaving Heaven, then in the abandonment He suffered on the cross. Her eyes stung. Thankful for Greg's little body shielding her from open view, she ducked her head and let the tears flow. Startled, she glanced sideways when Timothy pushed a large handkerchief into her hand. Compassion hovered there in his suspiciously bright eyes.

She had recovered by the time Lucy handed out the first package. The room quickly filled with excited chatter and abandoned wrapping string. Greg and Phillip were ecstatic over their trucks. "Thanks for choosing two different colors," Timothy murmured. "Squabbles will be much easier to settle this way."

Ida nodded with a grin. "I spend my days figuring out how to mediate childhood disputes."

Ruth's eyes lit up when she saw her gifts. "It's wonderful, Miss Thomas! Now I won't lose my writing. Maybe I can even keep a diary." She stood to hold the skirts against herself. "And I love the pretty new clothes."

Lucy reached toward Timothy with a small, awkward-looking package. "This is from Miss Thomas and myself."

Timothy cradled the bundle in his hands. "I don't know what to say."

"Just open it," Lucy urged.

Delight spread across his features as brown paper fell away. "I've always wanted to be able to do something like this. Where did you find it?" he asked, his voice gruff as he looked at Ida.

"Mr. Barry used to make them."

"And one of these days you'll have to get Ida to tell you the story behind this one," Lucy announced.

"I have it on good authority she's a marvelous story-teller."

Timothy gave Phillip a quick hug.

"We've heard much the same rumor," Lionel commented, ruffling Tommy's hair.

She felt embarrassed to be singled out, yet somehow also warmly accepted. Almost like part of the family. Lucy handed her two bundles from the rapidly shrinking pile. "It's your turn." One contained a long navy wool skirt from Lucy, and the other a blouse that Nina had made from a matching print. Then Lionel handed her another package. It appeared perfectly normal. Brown paper had been wrapped around a cardboard box, and careful printing on the paper read, "To Miss Thomas from the McEvan family." However, when she held it, she could feel something moving inside. She heard scratching and soft mewling. Pulling the paper away, she saw a tiny gray kitten.

"Do you like her, Miss Thomas?" Greg asked eagerly.

"Dad said we had to ask Mrs. Barry if a kitten would be allowed here, and she said yes," Phillip informed her.

Ida lifted the kitten out gently. The creature fit well in her cupped hands. "She's so tiny. How old is she?"

"Not quite six weeks," Ruth explained. "Dad said she probably wasn't quite old enough, but he figured you'd love her enough to make up the difference."

Timothy's face turned redder than it had when Greg had revealed his early morning trips to the schoolhouse. Ida looked back at the kitten to give him time to recover, his comment settling into her heart with a warm glow. "Of course I'll love her. Isn't she pretty, Lucy?"

All of the children gathered closely, each wanting a chance to touch the soft fur. "What should I name her?" Ida asked them.

Several suggestions were offered. Tommy suggested

"Rover," which David informed him was a dog's name. Nina quickly intervened with "Joybelle" before a fight could erupt.

"I like that!" Ida exclaimed. "She's a Christmas gift, so she ought to have a Christmassy sounding name. Would you mind if I called her Belle for short?"

"Not at all," Nina assured her. "Young Lionel, would you bring our gift from Grandma's bedroom?"

The boy returned quickly, carrying a woven basket. "We didn't know how to wrap it, so Grandma said we could keep it upstairs until you opened your other presents." He offered the basket to her. "It's from us, the Spencers, I mean."

Cradling Belle in her lap, which Greg had vacated in the excitement, Ida examined the basket. A soft pad lined the bottom, making it a perfect bed for her pet. "How did you know?"

"When Ruth told me what they were doing, I dropped a hint to Lionel and Nina. Quite simple, actually." Lucy giggled.

Ida resisted the tears pushing at her eyelids. She'd thought this Christmas would be lonely and painful. Instead, some of the finest people she'd ever met had taken her to their hearts and lavished both love and material gifts on her. When Lucy reached over the basket to give her a hug, she lost the battle. Lucy held her for several long moments, allowing Ida's tears to soak her shoulder. When the wave of emotion had passed, Ida pulled back. "I'm sorry."

"For what?" Lucy's eyes glistened, too.

"Christmas isn't supposed to be tearful."

Nina knelt awkwardly beside Ida to give a hug of her own. "Nonsense. Christmas is about love, and sometimes love brings tears."

Phillip pushed into the circle for a hug, then Greg, then

Tommy, then Tabby. Their enthusiastic embraces pulled a chuckle from Ida. "I have to be the most blessed teacher in the world to have students like you." She glanced at Nina and added, "And families like you, too."

"We're blessed to have you."

The gruff remark startled Ida, who'd forgotten Timothy seated beside her. She met his gaze directly for the first time that day, touched by the gentleness she saw there. "I just hope I'm worth your confidence."

"You already have been." He smiled at Ruth, who now sat against the wall with a dreamy look, running her fingers over the cloth covering her new diary.

Ida laughed softly. "It looks like genius is stirring." The veil of restraint she'd felt with him so far gradually lifted.

Dinner lasted well over an hour, as everyone lingered over the delicious food. At Lucy's insistence, Nina lumbered upstairs with Tabby for a dual nap. The men took the rest of the children into the sitting room so Lucy and Ida could clean the kitchen in peace.

With the last pot dried and put away, Ida joined the men and children. "Where's Mom?" Lionel inquired.

"She wanted a bit of a nap." Ida returned Phillip's ever-present hug.

Timothy grimaced at his two sons. "I wish a couple of people I know would make the same choice."

"Surely not with all the excitement in the air. We might miss something." Ida couldn't resist teasing him gently. He looked more peaceful than she'd ever seen him. His eyes even contained a hint of a twinkle.

"Read me a story," Greg demanded with a tug on her skirt.

"Please?" his father prompted.

"Please," the boy echoed dutifully.

"What story would you like?"

"This one." Tommy held up his Christmas gift.

Ida had no sooner seated herself on the sofa than small bodies crowded around her. Greg immediately claimed her lap, while Phillip and Tommy snuggled close on either side. Clara and David sat by her feet, leaning against the sofa. Young Lionel sat on the other side of Phillip, not wanting to be left out. Timothy smiled indulgently at the pile of little people. Ruth had found a pencil and was huddled in her familiar position against the wall, already intently writing in her new book. Lionel dozed in a chair in the opposite corner.

Ida packed as much expression into her reading as she could, her audience's affection pulling the drama out of her. Less than halfway into the story, she felt Greg go limp against her, his even breathing indicating he'd finally succumbed to weariness. As she turned a page, she glanced up at Timothy, who extended his arms in a silent offer to take Greg. She shook her head, not wanting to disturb the boy or change the quiet atmosphere surrounding her. Phillip and Tommy also dozed off before the story's end. Timothy and Lionel took the little ones upstairs, and the rest of the afternoon passed quickly in numerous games of pick-up sticks and tic-tac-toe with the older children. Lucy awoke in time to serve coffee and more pie before the men decided to take their families home. "The cows still expect to be milked, even on Christmas Day," Lionel explained. With hugs all around, the Spencer family departed.

Lucy went upstairs to fetch a second load of winter wraps. Ruth helped Phillip gather the family's gifts from the parlor, and Ida found herself alone with Timothy in the kitchen. He looked down at the sleeping child he'd just brought from the upstairs bedroom. "You've been really good for my children," he commented softly.

"It must be because I love them." She didn't know what else to say.

Some of the softness disappeared from his gaze. "Any child would be blessed to have you as a mother. From what I've heard, it won't be long before you and Mr. Danielson will be creating a family of your own."

Ida looked directly into his blue eyes, wishing she could remove the splinters of pain she still saw there. Her reply came without forethought. "Mr. Danielson knows my heart isn't available. I seem to have fallen in love with someone who already has a family." The words had hardly left her mouth when she realized what she'd said. Mortification overwhelmed her and she fled to her room without waiting for a response.

thirteen

For days afterward, Ida wished she could have retracted those words. What an unseemly thing to have said! She stroked Belle's downy fur and the kitten mewed as if in sympathy. *Why did Timothy McEvan's presence elicit emotional responses from her so contrary to good sense? If Mom had been here, she wouldn't have gotten so carried away,* she thought irrationally. Finally, Lucy cornered her. "Ida, you need to talk."

To her dismay, tears threatened to destroy her composure. She hadn't opened the subject before for fear she'd cry rather than talk. She shook her head.

Lucy grasped her hands. "You're just going to make yourself sick if you don't get this out where you can deal with it. Now what is it?"

The unusual sternness in her voice startled Ida into cooperation. She related the entire humiliating conversation, ending with, "I'm embarrassed, Lucy. How could I have been so forward?"

Silently Lucy gathered the weeping young woman into an embrace until the sobs ceased. "Ida, do you truly believe every detail of your life is under God's control?"

The answer came without thinking. "Yes."

"Including your mistakes?"

That question made Ida think. "I guess so."

Lucy nodded with a comforting smile. "Do you really believe that, or is it just the right answer for this quiz?"

"If He couldn't control my mistakes, He wouldn't really be

omnipotent." Ida smiled shakily.

"It sounds to me like you're convinced. May I tell you what I think about what happened?" Lucy poured out cups of steaming tea.

Ida nodded and wrapped her hands around the cup's warmth.

"I don't pretend to know what God has planned for you or Timothy. But I have noticed how well you compliment each other when you're not trying to pretend there's no attraction between you. You look to me like a perfect fit." Lucy's words created a warm gush of joy within Ida. "Maybe your admission was just what Timothy needs to encourage him to leave his grief and guilt behind."

Ida wanted to believe her friend, but one thought wouldn't go away. "My mother would have been horrified."

"You don't know that."

"She told me more times than I can count how important discretion is, how men don't respect women who let too much of their feelings show."

"Maybe Timothy isn't the only one who needs to leave a bit of the past behind."

The quiet comment stopped Ida's whirling thoughts mid-syllable. "What do you mean?"

Lucy again grasped Ida's hands. "From what you've said, I know your mother was a fine lady. But Ida, dear, she's now at home with the Lord she loved. You can't live the rest of your life wondering how she'd handle what you're facing. She taught you as well as she knew how. You now answer only to your Heavenly Father for the choices you make. You'll never go wrong asking yourself how to respond as He would."

It made sense to Ida. Yet, as she pondered the conversation over the next few days, she still resisted her loss. Acting contrary to what she remembered of her mother felt like betrayal. Through the mental clamor, she recalled Timothy's grief-filled eyes. Was she as reluctant as he to let go?

As had become habit, she discussed her thoughts with Lucy. "I'd never realized before how much Mom's opinions mattered to me."

"Of course they do." Lucy thumped her bread dough one last time, plopped it into a bowl, and set it near the stove to rise. "She was both your mother and your friend. The danger is when pleasing her becomes your sole reason for what you do."

"I've been reading Proverbs lately," Ida mused. "It talks as much about a person's heart as it does about actions."

The counter now clean, Lucy sat at the table across from Ida. "You're right. Jesus talked often about heart. He even went so far as to say that doing the right thing, such as keeping the law, with a wrong motivation makes the action wrong, too."

"I haven't been able to forget what you said about asking myself what Jesus would do. By always thinking about what Mom would do, I've made her more important than God."

"And in so doing, lost track of the beautiful uniqueness of yourself," Lucy replied gently.

Startled, Ida looked up from her tea questioningly.

Lucy smiled. "When God made you, He gave you certain characteristics for a purpose. Trying to be exactly like your Mom, Ida, says the way He made you isn't good enough."

Ida pondered for several moments. "I never thought of it that way. I've just been thinking in terms of making Mom proud of me if she were here."

Lucy patted Ida's hands in the familiar gesture. "From what you've said of your mom, I'm sure she's proud of you. Nothing makes a mother happier than to see her children becoming the people God meant them to be."

Despite her other personal discoveries, Ida still wondered about Timothy. She had seen him a couple of times in town, but his greeting was nothing more or less than that of a respectful acquaintance. She couldn't help wondering if their comfortable camaraderie of Christmas Day had vanished forever.

ঞ

The second Sunday of the year brought the coldest temperatures Ida had yet experienced. Lucy warned her to bundle up well for their trip to the Spencer farm. "As long as the wind isn't blowing, we'll be fine."

Ida donned three thick sweaters. The top one had been one of her first knitting projects and had turned out too large to be worn alone. At Mom's insistence, she'd kept the garment. With gratitude, she realized its size made a perfect fit over the rest of her clothing. By the time she met Lucy at the back door, they both wore so many layers they could hardly waddle. Ida giggled. "No one could accuse us of flaunting our figures."

Lionel met them at the barn almost before the buggy had stopped. "Ma, I was afraid you'd do this."

Lucy favored her son with a tolerant glance. "It's like I told Ida. If we let a little cold keep us at home, we won't budge until March."

"But what if something had happened? You'd freeze to death."

"Not as long as we're walking." She allowed him to help her down, then patted his arm. "Thanks for your concern, Son, but I've lived in this country long enough to know when it's dangerous. If we'd had any wind, I would have kept us at home."

"Just hurry inside, please, and I'll take care of the horse."

From Lionel's reaction, Ida wondered if anyone else would brave the weather. However, it appeared most people shared Lucy's perspective. The pile of blankets, sweaters, coats, and other winter wear in the corner grew to mammoth proportions as each family arrived. She greeted Cynthia Pierce enthusiastically. "I'm so glad to see you. Theo told me you'd not been feeling well since Christmas."

Cynthia returned her hug. "It always happens when I let myself get overtired. Hopefully, I'll be able to make it to school this next week."

"Much as I appreciate your help, please don't push yourself unnecessarily."

"She won't," Doug assured her, putting an arm around his wife's shoulders.

Lionel started singing, accompanied by his guitar. Conversation stilled to a minimum as everyone found seats. Ida chose a place beside Lucy. When a blast of frigid air behind them indicated more arrivals, she knew without looking who had come. Her suspicions were confirmed when a well-clothed small person clambered into her lap uninvited. "Hi, Teacher. We comed even though Daddy said it was almost too cold," Phillip informed her in a stage whisper.

She put a finger on his lips to shush him while she removed his coat and other winter gear. "Go put these on the pile, and then you can come back and sit with me if your dad says it's okay." Since the youngster rejoined her quickly, she assumed he obtained permission. She refused to let herself look for Timothy to confirm. However, she found herself unable to concentrate on the songs they sang.

Lionel eventually stood and put his guitar to one side. "Your presence here today is encouraging to my wife and I. Though

we would have condemned no one for staying home, your
being here in spite of the weather lets us know these afternoons of worship together are just as important to you as they
are to us. I didn't prepare anything to talk about today, so
I'm wondering if anyone else has something."

After a brief pause, Ida heard a rustle behind her. "Yes,
Lionel, I think I do." To her amazement, Timothy strode to
the front of the room. "I'm not much good at talking in front
of people, but you people have been so good to me and my
children, I feel like you're family." He cleared his throat,
then sat on the chair Lionel had vacated. "I'd like to start
with a Scripture reading. Lamentations chapter three, verses
22 through 26." Ida noticed his fingers trembling as he found
the passage in his Bible. "'It is of the LORD'S mercies that
we are not consumed, because his compassions fail not. They
are new every morning: great is thy faithfulness. The LORD
is my portion, saith my soul; therefore will I hope in him.
The LORD is good unto them that wait for him, to the soul
that seeketh him. It is good that a man should both hope and
quietly wait for the salvation of the LORD.'"

He cleared his throat a couple more times before continuing. Ida felt like she sat on the edge of an important discovery, and silently prayed he'd have the composure to say all he
wanted to say. "Eighteen months ago, my wife and three of
my children drowned. I've blamed both God and myself. In
my anger, I almost committed myself to never being whole
again. As a result, I haven't been a very good neighbor or
father. But you people refused to let me bury myself in bitterness." He looked at Doug Pierce, and for a moment Ida
thought he would break down completely. He swallowed hard.
"Through you I've realized remaining angry at God was
cutting me off from my only true Source of comfort and

healing." Now his gaze met Ida's. Rather than looking away in embarrassment, she found she wanted to be able to see all the way into his soul, to realize the depth of what he was trying to say. "You've also provided the love and guidance my children needed while I found my way back to my Heavenly Father. I've seen the faith and courage with which you face your heartaches, and it has challenged me to do the same. Just before Christmas, I opened Janet's Bible for the first time since the river." He had to pause for a couple of moments. "This passage I've read to you was underlined. It seemed to be a message to me, both from Janet and from my Heavenly Father. I will probably never be able to explain why God allowed half our family to be swept away. But I've come to know that His love for us is no different than it was before. He's been waiting for me to let Him show me how to cope and heal. We as a family will always miss Janet, Daniel, Sam, and Benjamin. But because of the healing I've decided to accept, we're now ready to let them go, knowing they're waiting for us in a better place. It's up to us who are left to make the most of the future God has put before us." His gaze traveled around the room, making eye contact with each person there, then returned to Ida. "We'll continue to need your love and prayers, even as we thank you for what you've already done." He sat down.

Silence gripped the room. Then Doug thumped over to Timothy to enfold him in a great bear hug. Lionel followed. Their wives sat smiling and crying at the same time. Even Kate Harper seemed touched. Ida became aware of the tears trickling down her own cheeks. She'd felt Timothy's pain; now she'd experienced his first steps toward healing. It wouldn't be an easy path to travel, but at least he'd found the One who would make it possible.

fourteen

When Ida awoke Monday morning, her first conscious thought was of Timothy. A prayer of thanksgiving bubbled from her heart. "Thank you, Father, that he's found You again." *How Mom would have rejoiced! But then, Mom had never met Timothy.* The familiar twist of pain shadowed Ida's joy. Remembering the solace he had found in Lamentations, Ida quickly readied herself for the new day so she could spend a few moments studying the passage again. " . . . his compassions fail not. They are new every morning . . ." She read the verses a second and a third time.

The clattering of stove lids in the kitchen told her Lucy was up, too. She grabbed her Bible and raced out to share her discovery. "Lucy, listen to this!"

"Good morning to you, too." Lucy's eyes twinkled. "Let me guess. You've been reading Lamentations."

Ida smiled self-consciously. "Yes. And I found something I've never seen before." She read the verses aloud. "It seems like every morning when I get up, I have to face all over again the fact that Mom's not here." Lucy nodded understandingly, but didn't interrupt. "It's like the grief is fresh each day. But these verses say God's compassion is also new every morning. It's almost like He matches His compassion to my hurt."

Lucy's eyes moistened. "That's beautiful, Ida. I don't know how many times I've read those verses, but I hadn't understood them that way before."

Grumbling from the opposite doorway brought their conversation to a halt. "How's a working man supposed to get

144

his rest with you two wimen blabbering all the time?"

"Good morning, Mr. Carey," Lucy responded. "You're just in time for fresh coffee."

"Might as well have something to get me going since you made sure I can't sleep." He winked subtly at Ida.

She almost gasped. While she'd grown accustomed to his complaining, she'd always thought he was serious. At least this morning, it seemed he was simply acting to see what reaction he'd get out of Lucy.

"But morning's the best time of the day." Lucy set a steaming mug in front of him. "Maybe if you spent more time enjoying it, you wouldn't be so grouchy the rest of the day."

"What have I told you about tryin' to run my life?" he growled.

"Just a helpful suggestion," she replied innocently, grinning at Ida when he wasn't looking.

But even the playful bickering couldn't take away Ida's wonder at her discovery. She and Mom had read through the Bible together many times. Somehow, there always seemed to be a new personal message in it from her Heavenly Father.

❧

The next few days at school were hectic. The students hadn't yet settled back into routine. In addition, Dawson Creek's first train was due to arrive Thursday evening. The excitement that gripped the entire town also invaded her classroom. She dismissed her students early Thursday afternoon so everyone could get chores done and supper eaten before the locomotive's arrival.

To her astonishment, Mr. Carey met her and Misty as they entered the barn. He appeared to be feeding Lucy's horse and cleaning out stalls. "I'll rub her down for you, ma'am."

"Thank you, Mr. Carey."

"I wasn't doin' nuthin' anyway," he excused himself gruffly.

"Just don't expect me to do it all the time."

She thought she caught a glimpse of his roguish twinkle, but couldn't be sure. On her way through the kitchen, she paused to whisper to Lucy, "You'll never guess who's out in the barn."

"He came home from work about an hour ago, madder than a wet cat they'd closed the store early. He devoured pie and coffee, then disappeared out the back door."

"He did warn me not to expect this of him all the time."

Lucy grinned. "I don't think he has anything to worry about."

"How long before supper?"

"The train's due at six, so I thought we'd eat in about thirty minutes. I'd like to leave for the station early."

"I'll be out to help in a few minutes," Ida promised as she closed her bedroom door. She quickly shook the chalk dust out of her black wool skirt, then removed her riding clothes. For the evening's activity, she wanted something festive-looking. Her Christmas gift from Lucy seemed just right. Her outfit would be covered by her shawl, she reminded herself. It didn't matter. She felt like dressing up, so she would.

A crowd had already gathered by the time Lucy and Ida arrived. Thankfully the temperature had warmed enough to make waiting outside possible. Several people moved aside so the two ladies could get closer to the front.

"Hello, Mrs. Barry and Miss Thomas," Mrs. Danielson smiled at them as they found a place to stand. "Isn't this a wonderful evening?"

Lucy returned the greeting. Surprise took away Ida's power of speech. She hadn't expected pleasantness from the Danielsons after what had happened between her and Ken. She scanned the crowd, but didn't see him. A tackle around her knees almost sent her tumbling, while a firm grip on her elbow steadied her. She grinned down at Phillip. "I'm glad to see you, too." Timothy's hand lingered a moment longer than necessary, which she found strangely pleasant. "Thank you, Mr. McEvan."

He chuckled. "It's the least I can do until my son learns how to say hello less exuberantly."

Greg leaned from his dad's arm to give Ida a hug, bringing her into even closer contact with Timothy. She directed her attention toward Ruth, accompanied as usual by Theo. "What do you think of us getting our own train?"

"Dad says now that we have regular shipments from the city, we might even get a lending library. Do you think so, Miss Thomas?" The girl's eyes sparkled.

"It's possible. What do you think, Theo?"

"It would be wonderful. The train will also make it easier for me to come home for visits after I start medical school."

"I'm sure your mother likes that idea." Ida smiled at Cynthia, standing just behind her son.

A distant whistle interrupted conversation, causing a rumble of excitement through the crowd as everyone strained forward to see down the tracks. More quickly than seemed possible, the black smoking engine roared up to the tiny station building, pulling several freight cars and a passenger car behind it. Several railroad dignitaries disembarked. The new stationmaster shook hands importantly.

"What's she doing here?"

Ida barely heard Timothy's muttered exclamation, though she felt his tension behind her. She looked back toward the passenger car, where a well-dressed woman hesitated at the top of the steps, loathe to contaminate herself with what she saw around her. Her gaze swept through the crowded yard almost unseeingly, until she found Timothy. At once, her face hardened. She moved toward them purposefully.

"Mother Carrington! How kind of you to visit us." Timothy strode forward, greeting her with more warmth than Ida felt the lady's expression deserved. "Ruth, Phillip, and Greg, this is your Grandmother Carrington, your mother's mother."

Phillip clutched Ida's leg more tightly, while Greg ducked his head into his father's shoulder. Only Ruth appeared willing to become acquainted. "Hello, Grandmother. I'm glad you're here."

"Well, I'm not." Mrs. Carrington lifted her nose as if smelling something disagreeable. "I've come to take you children back to Toronto where you can be cared for properly. I would have come much sooner, but I didn't fancy riding in an open wagon or an outdated truck from that hamlet they call Hythe."

Ida watched the man she loved age abruptly. The grief lines which had been fading around his mouth and eyes deepened. He looked at her, helpless agony in his expression. She held out her hand to the uninvited guest. "Mrs. Carrington, I'm Ida Thomas, the children's school teacher. You would be more than welcome to spend the night at the boardinghouse where I live. Tomorrow we'll take you out to the farm so you and your family can discuss your plans in private." She didn't know where the words came from, but they brought a light of gratitude to Timothy's stricken eyes.

Mrs. Carrington didn't thaw a bit. "I suppose that's my only option, since no train departs this Godforsaken place tonight. Timothy, be sure your children's bags are packed when I arrive tomorrow. From their appearance now, I'll be ashamed to have them seen in Toronto, but they will need something to wear until they get there." She looked imperiously at Ida. "If you'll direct your driver and carriage over here, I'll get that stationmaster to bring my bags out."

Ida mustered her most courteous smile. "I'm afraid we don't have a driver or a carriage. If you'd like to walk with

Mrs. Barry and me back to the boardinghouse, I'm sure Mr. McEvan will be happy to bring your bags in the wagon."

Mingled fear and fury showed in the lady's face. "I should have known Timothy would bring my precious daughter and grandchildren to some place so primitive. In Toronto, no true lady is seen walking anywhere."

Lucy's reappearance saved Ida from an unwise answer. "Mrs. Carrington, this is Mrs. Barry, the lady who owns the boardinghouse. Lucy, this is Mrs. Carrington, Mr. McEvan's mother-in-law."

Lucy extended her hand in greeting. "We're glad to have you with us."

Mrs. Carrington ignored the hand. "I'm certainly not glad to be here." She expanded on the theme throughout the short walk downtown. The buildings were ugly, the weather sharp enough to ruin a lady's complexion, the paths shoveled through the snow far too narrow, and the piles of horse droppings offensive in the extreme. "Why you people don't invest in something clean and sensible like automobiles, I'll never know." Her mood didn't improve when they reached the boardinghouse. No carpeting, no powder room, no indoor "privacy room," and so the list continued.

Ida had never admired her friend and landlady so much as during that interminable evening. Though nothing provided for their guest was good enough, Lucy remained gracious and attentive.

The following morning brought no relief. Mrs. Carrington wanted to set out immediately after breakfast, in spite of Lucy's insistence that they wait for daylight. Ida saddled Misty and rode out of the yard with a feeling of guilty relief. At least she could escape to school.

She recognized Pierce's team in the shelter as she approached, then Cynthia came running out of the schoolhouse.

"Ida, would you let me take classes for you this morning so you can go over to McEvans'?"

Surprise stole Ida's reply. Finally, she found a coherent thought. "Why? Has someone been hurt?"

Cynthia shook her head. "Doug and I were talking about it last night, after watching what happened at the train station. Both of us think you could help Timothy just by being there."

Ida had felt the same way since awaking, but it seemed horribly presumptuous. "Won't he think I'm interfering?"

"I think he'll be grateful for the support. We'll be praying for you."

Ida held Misty still for several more moments. Mom would be horrified that she'd even contemplated arriving uninvited at a single man's residence. But that thought was quickly replaced by another. What would God's compassion have her do? She smiled at Cynthia. "Thanks for the offer. I just hope we're doing the right thing."

She guided Misty automatically down the winding trail to McEvans' farm. Two bundled figures ahead in the pre-dawn shadows caught her attention. She reigned the horse to a stop and dismounted to talk to them. "How are you two this morning?"

The usually voluble Phillip had nothing to say. Ruth explained. "He's afraid Grandmother is going to convince Dad we have to go with her."

"That's understandable," Ida replied, kneeling in the snow and holding out her arms to the silent boy. "Would a hug help?"

Phillip ran into her with such force she almost toppled over. He buried his head into her scarf as sobs started to shake his small body. "She can't make us leave, can she, Teacher? I don't want to go away from you or my Dad or the horses and cows and chickens. How does Daddy know she's really our grandmother? Maybe she's just a horrid old lady who steals children."

She hugged him tightly through their layers of winter clothing until he calmed enough to listen. "Do you really think your Daddy would let you go anywhere that wasn't good for you?"

"But she didn't ask him." He hiccuped. "She told him, and he didn't say no."

"But he didn't say yes, either, did he?"

"No." Phillip sniffed loudly. "I think I need a hanky."

Ruth pulled one from the cloth bag that carried her books and their lunch. "What do you think, Miss Thomas? Is he really going to let her take us away?"

Ida stood to put her arms around the girl. "I don't know, Ruth. The only thing I do know is that God isn't going to stop taking care of you now. Would it help if I prayed with you?"

Both nodded, their eyes filled with a trust so sincere it brought tears to her own. She bowed her head, while hugging them both close. "Lord Jesus, Ruth and Phillip are worried this morning because they don't know what their dad is going to decide. We know you know their grandmother wants to take them back to Toronto, and they don't want to leave. Will you please give them peace today so they can learn well, and give their dad wisdom as he makes his decision? In Jesus' name, Amen."

The two hugged her again, then suddenly seemed to realize which direction she'd been riding. "Aren't you going to school this morning?" Ruth asked.

Even for these two, Ida felt embarrassed to explain. "Mrs. Pierce offered to take classes for me this morning. She and Mr. Pierce think I can help your dad. Do you think so?" She appealed to Ruth for confirmation.

The teenager didn't even hesitate. "Yes. He doesn't know

it yet, but he needs you."

Ida didn't dare explore further. "Then I'd better see what I can do. You'll be good for Mrs. Pierce, won't you, Phillip?"

"Yes, ma'am." He flashed his usual fun-filled grin at her, then trudged off through the snow behind his sister.

He needs you . . . the thought wouldn't complete itself, nor would it leave. *What had led Ruth to such a conclusion?* Timothy had made great strides in dealing with his grief, but was he really ready to admit another woman to his life? The sight of him entering the barn ahead made her put her contemplations aside.

"Daddy, look who's here!"

She heard Greg's happy announcement as he followed his dad. Abruptly, Timothy came back out. Relief gentled his expression when he saw her. "What brings the schoolteacher here?" He reached up to help her dismount.

How could she explain without seeming forward? "The Pierces and I thought you could use some moral support this morning."

"Cynthia's at school?" The gentleness in his eyes didn't change.

Ida nodded. "I met Ruth and Phillip on the way."

"He's pretty upset, isn't he?"

"Probably no more than you are."

He didn't answer until he'd put Misty into a stall with fresh hay. "She can offer them so much more than I can."

Ida knew if she pursued his thoughts further, she could be accused of meddling. Yet she felt compelled. "Like what?"

He scooped Greg onto his shoulders. "Nice clothes, higher education, all the advantages of city living."

"Mr. McEvan." Though she thought of him as Timothy, she carefully didn't let it slip. "Would you mind telling me why you and your wife came out west?"

He looked at her intently for several long moments, then shifted his gaze off into the distance. "We wanted our children to learn—" His voice trailed off as if he couldn't find the words to explain himself.

"Independence?" She made the guess from what she knew of his character.

"In part." He nodded slowly. After a few moments' contemplation, he continued. "Janet often said city living encourages people to forget God's simplicity."

She sensed the process of putting his thoughts into words would help him make a decision. "I think I understand, but can you explain a little more?"

"Like this." He waved toward the gradually lighting horizon. "City folk are often too busy to watch the sun come up. They never pay attention to the seasons except to complain about the hardship of rain or snow. They don't think about where their food comes from. We wanted our children to enjoy what they eat because they helped plant and harvest it. Am I making sense?" He finally looked at her again.

She nodded, amazed at the sheer quantity of words he'd used. *Had she said enough? Too much?* Lucy's favorite verse came to mind. "The steps of a good woman are ordered by the Lord..." Leaning against one of the stalls, she watched him ponder and remember. *"Father, he needs to feel your presence like he never has before,"* she prayed silently.

The jangle of harness coming toward them punctured the quietly intent mood. "Here she comes." He touched her arm. "I'm glad you're here. Would you hold onto Greg while I unhitch the horse? And please keep praying."

She held out her arms and the toddler tumbled into them. How had Timothy known she was praying? His perception gave her an odd feeling of intimacy with him. He helped his mother-in-law out of the buggy.

"That lady's mad at Daddy."

Greg's whispered confidence startled Ida. She glanced at Mrs. Carrington, whose disapproving countenance hadn't altered since breakfast.

If Lucy was surprised to see Ida at the farm, she didn't let on. She beckoned, strain showing in fine lines around her eyes. "Maybe Greg and I could play out here in the barn."

Greg bounced excitedly in Ida's arms. Ida smiled at him, then at Lucy. "That's a great idea."

Lucy accepted Timothy's assistance in getting out of the buggy, then held out her arms for the small boy. "If you don't mind, Mr. McEvan, Greg and I will stay out here and talk with the horses. With the door closed, we'll keep nice and warm."

Timothy looked up from the harnesses he had unhitched. "Much obliged, Mrs. Barry."

Mrs. Carrington barely gave him time to turn the horse into the corral before demanding, "Well, are you going to leave me out here to freeze?"

"No, Mother. Come inside and I'll brew us all a pot of hot tea." Timothy motioned the two ladies ahead of him into the small log cabin.

For once, Mrs. Carrington remained silent, though she inspected her surroundings carefully. "I wouldn't have expected you to do this well without Janet, Timothy." Her tone made sure Timothy didn't think he'd been given a compliment.

"Ruth has been a fine little housekeeper." Timothy responded as if he had been commended.

"That's my point exactly," Mrs. Carrington exclaimed. "All that girl should be thinking about is party dresses and hairstyles, not trying to turn this hovel into a home."

"When you saw her last night did she appear unhappy, Mother?"

"Don't call me Mother." The woman sat up straighter, if that were possible. "You lost all relationship to me when you killed my daughter. I'm only here to rescue my three remaining grandchildren from your foolishness."

Pain knifed through Timothy's face at the accusation, but peace quickly replaced it. "It doesn't matter what you think of me, Mrs. Carrington. I'll always love you because you raised the woman I loved. For awhile, I blamed myself for her death, but I don't anymore. In time, you won't either."

"Sentiment isn't going to change my mind, Mr. McEvan. The fact remains that my grandchildren no longer have a mother. It's my duty to make sure they're well cared for."

"I don't agree." Timothy's voice remained calm.

Obviously, few people dared disagree with Mrs. Carrington. She seemed shocked into silence, if only briefly. "And what can you provide for them that I can't? You've already deprived them and me of my daughter."

"No one has mourned my wife's death more than I." Timothy set his cup down on the table and stood as if to shake off invisible bonds. "Nevertheless, I'm as much the children's father as she was their mother. We're still a family even though four of us are no longer present. Our family love hasn't changed."

"Noble thoughts, Mr. McEvan, but they won't give my grandchildren the finer things of life which they deserve."

"Fancy clothes can't replace love, Mother."

"Your so-called love didn't keep my daughter alive."

"And you want to punish me by taking our children away." Timothy turned to face his mother-in-law directly.

Mrs. Carrington didn't deny the charge.

"I know you loved Janet. Breaking her children's hearts isn't going to bring her back."

"The children will adapt. When they realize what I can

offer them, they won't even look back."

"Yes, they will, Mother. Janet and I brought our family out here because we wanted more for them than we felt city life could offer. They've become part of this farm. You won't be able to transplant them back."

"You can't raise them without a mother."

"I don't intend to try."

Mrs. Carrington seemed to become aware of Ida's presence for the first time. Ida willed herself not to blush under the woman's squint-eyed scrutiny. Timothy's words had fanned a flame of hope within her, but she couldn't afford to let her countenance reveal it. Mrs. Carrington looked back at Timothy. "What woman in her right mind would move into this place and take on three children just to marry you?"

"The right one," Timothy answered calmly.

Mrs. Carrington made a sound that in a less cultured person would have been a snort. "You always were a dreamer. I'll make a compromise with you. I'll take Ruth and you can keep the two boys. I wouldn't know what to do with them anyway."

Ida bit back her protest at the lady's callous disposal of Phillip and Greg. Timothy's quick glance reminded her that any input from her would strengthen Mrs. Carrington's determination.

"Mother Carrington, you are not taking even one of my children. God gave them to Janet and me. Since Janet's gone, it's now my responsibility, and mine alone, to care for them."

"They're all I have left of my daughter. Can't you understand that? I tried to get here as soon as I received your letter, but as you well know, there was no civilized means of travel to your town until yesterday." Her tone implied that Timothy could have done something about it had he wished. "With

Ruth to remind me of her, maybe I'll be able to forgive you for what you've done."

Timothy's lips whitened. His eyes turned steely gray. "My children are not for sale, for any price. I've forgiven myself for the river accident. Whether you ever do or not is your choice. In any case, you're not taking Janet's daughter away from me."

A spot of bright colour appeared above each of Mrs. Carrington's sharp cheekbones. "Are you denying me contact with my own grandchildren?"

"You know I would never do that." Timothy refilled the teacups. "You may write to them as often as you like, and I'll encourage them to reply to your letters. If you want to invite them to come live with you when they finish school, I'll let them make their own decisions. Until then, they remain with me on the farm Janet wanted for them."

Mrs. Carrington didn't say anything for awhile. Finally she stood and fastened the coat she'd refused to remove. "May God forgive you for breaking my heart. I know I can't. If you should change your mind before the train leaves this afternoon, you know where to find me."

fifteen

Mrs. Carrington slammed the door behind her as she sailed out. Timothy turned to Ida, his sagging shoulders beginning to straighten. "Who is going to tell her the train doesn't leave until next week?"

"I guess Lucy will have to." Ida noticed his mischievous smile closely resembled Phillip's. He finally looked released from an overwhelming weight.

His expression sobered. "I can't tell you how much I appreciate your being here, Miss Thomas."

"I didn't do much."

"You prayed." His tone told her how much he'd relied on it. "From the first time I met you, I noticed the way peace hovers around you. It rescued me today."

If she hadn't watched the battle of emotions on his face during the past hour, his description would have seemed melodramatic. She knew he'd just fought for a life beyond grief and guilt. "One of my favorite Scripture passages says God wants to give us peace like a river. Maybe He wanted to show you today that His river can give as much as another river took away."

"He gives more, Miss Thomas, much, much more." With that enigmatic statement, he held her cape for her. "Mrs. Barry could probably use my help hitching up the buggy."

"And I should return to my classroom."

"Thank Mrs. Pierce for me, will you please? I don't know if I could have handled Mother without you." His hands rested on her shoulders after he settled her cape into place, leaving a

158

tingling warmth after he reached for the door. They walked in silence to the barn, where Lucy led the horse from the corral. Mrs. Carrington's usual stream of complaints had dried up for the moment.

Ida and Timothy waved the two ladies off down the lane, then Timothy saddled Misty. "Your horse certainly is beautiful, Miss Thomas." He patted Misty's nose.

"She's actually just on loan to me from Nina Spencer. It's been wonderful to be able to ride to school, especially after the town moved." She accepted his help up into the saddle, while Greg watched from a nearby pile of clean hay. "Have a great day helping your dad, Greg."

Greg grinned at being acknowledged. He pulled his thumb from his mouth long enough to wave. "Bye, Miss Thomas."

Phillip and Ruth detached themselves from the group milling in the yard for recess. Ida realized she should have asked Timothy what to tell them. "What happened?" Ruth inquired, while Phillip wondered, "Is that lady taking us with her?"

"Let me get Misty put away, then we'll talk." Ida laughed, hoping to reassure them. When the horse had been taken care of, she knelt in the snow outside the shelter so she would be on Phillip's eye level. "Phillip, who is supposed to decide whether or not you leave?"

He didn't hesitate. "Daddy."

"That's right. So would it be fair of me to tell before he's had a chance to talk with you?"

Phillip ducked his head. "I guess not."

Ida glanced up at Ruth, then tipped Phillip's head up so she could look into his face. "I know you're both worried. I would be, too, if I were you. Just remember, we talked to Jesus about it this morning, and the Bible tells us He makes everything work out the way that is best for us."

The shadow of fear lifted from Ruth's eyes first, then a

sunny smile broke out on her brother's face. "I'd better go play before Mrs. Pierce rings the bell."

By day's end, Ida felt grateful Cynthia had stayed beyond the morning. For some reason Ida didn't want to investigate, she seemed unable to concentrate. Usually she had no trouble listening to the first graders read while keeping an eye on the middle grades in case someone got fidgety and watching for signs of difficulty among the older students. Today it was all she could do to keep her mind focused on the lesson being recited. "I don't know what I would have done without you," she told Cynthia after the last student left. "I wouldn't have been much use alone."

Cynthia smiled gently. "I expected that. Was it too awful this morning?"

Ida checked to make sure no young ears hovered too closely, and lowered her voice to a whisper. "I think it actually brought out the best in Mr. McEvan. I've never seen him more confident. She accused him of killing her daughter, and he refused to accept the blame."

"He's come a long way this winter," Cynthia observed. "You've done more for him in five months than Doug has been able to do in almost two years."

"Me?" Ida stared at her friend in amazement. "What have I had to do with it?"

"I don't know for sure, but you've certainly made a difference."

Ida just shook her head.

Cynthia tied her parka hood. "I don't think God is finished with you in Timothy McEvan's life. See you Sunday, if not before."

Ida stared at the closed door for a long time. Cynthia's comment made the second mention today of the deepening relationship between her and their neighbor. Ida knew her feelings for the widower hadn't made sense from the beginning. According to Ruth's earlier observation, the attraction was mutual. Timothy himself had as much as told his mother-in-law he was considering remarriage. Could it be possible?

She didn't pay much attention to Misty's progress on their way home. Her mind tumbled with possibilities. Nearing town, Ida realized trying to figure out what might happen would simply make her miserable. She prayed silently. "Father God, I don't know what Your plan is for Timothy and me. I've prayed for him as You directed, and I've done for him what I felt You wanted me to do when he turned to me for help. You know how much I care about him and his children. I trust You to accomplish your best in all of our lives. Please help me not to worry about it any more." Peace gradually settled over her thoughts.

Ruth and Phillip met her early the next morning at the warm schoolhouse, where a fire blazed as usual in the barrel stove. Their faces beamed. "Dad told us we don't have to go," Phillip stated unnecessarily, and threw his arms around Ida's neck in a stranglehold. "I'm so glad I don't have to go away from you."

"How do you feel, Ruth?" Ida looked over Phillip's head at his older sister.

"Relieved, and glad to see Dad looking so happy. He's acting really different, and he even whistles like he used to before . . ." her voice trailed off.

"Isn't it strange how some things can be like they used to, while other things will never be the same?" Ida asked softly.

Ruth's eyes softened. "I guess you kind of know what it's like."

That was Ida's only bright spot in the next four grueling days. Mrs. Carrington resented every moment standing between her and the next train out of the Peace River country.

Though it hardly seemed possible, she became more critical and demanding each day. Belle found herself confined to the bedroom after Mrs. Carrington's shriek of horror at discovering the kitten roamed the house at will. The second evening, Mr. Carey didn't even stay at the table long enough to eat dessert. He excused himself with a nod toward Lucy and Ida that clearly excluded Mrs. Carrington. "Pardon me, ladies. I'm sure your pie would be right tasty, Mrs. Barry, but my innards aren't workin' right tonight. Not that your cooking is a'tall responsible," he added before shutting his door with an emphatic thud.

Ida and Lucy had all they could do to keep their expressions appropriately sober. Mrs. Carrington quickly filled the brief silence. "What a rude man! I'm surprised you have any business at all, Mrs. Barry, if you allow creatures like that to eat at your table."

Tuesday afternoon, a strange silence shrouded the boardinghouse when Ida came home from school. She tiptoed into the kitchen, where she found Lucy at the table with a cup of tea and her Bible. "It's so quiet," she whispered.

Lucy smiled. "I know. I've been enjoying it ever since the train left at noon." Her eyes turned wistful. "I just wish Mrs. Carrington could discover how good God wants to be to her, if she'll let Him."

"Sometimes I forget that myself," Ida admitted, cuddling Belle, who was purring delightedly at being released from confinement. "I know how I want things to turn out and I forget to trust Him." She reflected on the number of times in the past few days she'd felt frustrated over Timothy. They had chatted briefly on Sunday, but Ida saw no clues to confirm Ruth's and Cynthia's comments. Disappointment clutched at her each time she remembered. Each time it became easier to turn her thoughts into prayers for the man she'd come to love.

Lucy nodded understandingly. "You're not alone in that, dear. How would you like to join me here with your Bible? I've missed our morning discussions."

Quiet confidence seeped into Ida's soul during that hour. It stayed with her during the rest of the week at school, even when Ruth handed her a note on Thursday afternoon. "Dad asked me to give this to you this morning, and I forgot until now. I'm sorry."

"That's all right." She gave the girl a quick hug. "I'm sure it's nothing serious. Are you studying with Theo this afternoon?"

Ruth shook her head. "Dad asked me to come straight home. He needs me to keep the boys inside while he takes care of something. He didn't say what."

"He'll let you know if it's important," Ida reassured her. She waited until the last student had disappeared down the road before opening the paper that seemed to burn in her hand.

Dear Miss Thomas,

Please do me the honor of waiting at the schoolhouse after the children leave. I need to ask you something.

Timothy McEvan

She studied the masculine scrawl. *Why here? Why not at church on Sunday, or the boardinghouse this evening? All I can do is wait,* she reminded herself. Knowing she wouldn't be able to concentrate on grading the older students' essays, she dipped some warm water from the pot on the back of the stove and began scrubbing desktops. The students probably wouldn't notice the difference, but it would keep her busy.

Half a dozen clean desks later, she heard a knock at the door. Timothy entered uncertainly. He looked reassured to see her there. "Thanks for waiting."

"I'm glad to help when I can." The words sounded stiff and formal, but what else could she say?

He cleared his throat several times before he could speak. "Miss Thomas, I feel like a fool for coming to you this way, but the more I pray about it, the more it seems like the right thing to do. Not that I don't want to; it just feels awkward since we haven't done hardly any courting." He stopped and studied the floor.

Ida slowly realized what he seemed to be trying to say. She waited, afraid he'd change his mind before he finished.

"The more I try to lead up to it easy-like, the more of a muddle I make." He looked straight into her eyes for the first time. "Miss Thomas, would you marry me?"

She felt like someone had just pulled the floor out from under her. While she'd hoped and prayed, she hadn't expected results this suddenly. Before she gave the answer she'd had waiting since Christmas, she wanted to hear something else. "Why?"

His expression didn't change, but she saw hurt in his eyes. "I'm sorry. I shouldn't have been—"

She grabbed his arm as he started to turn away. "I haven't answered you yet, Timothy." Her use of his name brought hope back into his face. "I have to know something first, though. Why do you want to marry me?"

"I need you," he stated simply.

Once again, she thought she knew what he meant, but she wanted to hear him say it before she committed herself. "Because you told your mother-in-law you'd find a mother for your children?"

It took a moment for her meaning to reach him. When it did, the tenderness she'd been watching for dawned in his eyes. He grasped both her hands with his farm-roughened fingers and looked directly into her eyes. "I need you more than they do." He stopped, as though searching for just the right words. "Your faith gave me courage to find God again. Your gentle spirit has helped me find peace." Uncertainty clouded his face. "I'm still not saying it right."

"Why, Timothy, that was almost eloquent!" she teased gently, knowing he needed reassurance before his confidence totally crumbled. Yet she still felt compelled to search for more. "Are you sure friendship isn't enough?"

He dropped her hands with a helpless sigh. "I'm sure." He looked into her eyes again. "I need you with me for always, or at least as long as God leaves us both on earth."

His last words reminded Ida of the difficult path he'd come, and the hurdles still facing him. "How can you be certain? It hasn't been that long since you lost Janet." She didn't want to hurt him by seeming reluctant, but she had to know his heart.

He claimed her hands once more. "In June, it will have been two long years. I'm finally ready to let myself care again. Christmas Day, you said you'd fallen in love with someone who has a family, and I've dared to hope I'm the one. Have you changed your mind?"

She felt the heat creeping up her neck and cheeks while she shook her head. "You don't know how often I've wished I hadn't said that."

"If you hadn't, I probably wouldn't be standing here now."

She looked into his eyes, waiting for the explanation. "Why?"

"I don't have much to offer a bride. My farm isn't much yet. I have three children who can be difficult. We're always going to remember and talk about Janet, Daniel, Sam, and Benjamin. In other words, I'm just a poor widower with three children and a lot of memories. You gave me hope we could be a whole family again."

Ida pulled her hands free so she could wrap her arms around him. "I'm just an orphaned schoolteacher with a lot of memories. I guess that's why I loved you so quickly."

He slowly returned her embrace. "Say that again," he whispered into her hair.

"I love you, Timothy McEvan."

"Does that mean you'll marry me?" He smiled gently, his eyes twinkling like Phillip's.

She teased him back. "Only if you love me, too."

A solid glow replaced the twinkles. "Always."

sixteen

Ida peeked out from behind the curtain that had been strung across one corner of the "meeting cabin" at Spencer's farm. Just as quickly, Lucy pulled her back. "Stop that! He'll see you," she whispered fiercely.

"How can he? He isn't here," Ida whispered back.

Lucy pulled Ida around to face her. "Ida Thomas, it's still ten minutes before the ceremony is to start, and you know how muddy these roads are with spring run-off. Timothy isn't going to change his mind now."

Ida forced a smile. "I know. I just want to see him."

Lucy adjusted the long, filmy veil. "After today, you'll be able to do just that every day for the rest of your lives. Shush now and calm yourself."

For the first time in three days, Ida allowed herself to sit idle. Nina and Cynthia had decided school should be canceled Friday to allow her time to finish preparations for her wedding, as well as to get her belongings moved to the McEvan farm. She and Lucy had finished her rose-toned wedding dress on Friday. Ida had felt the colored fabric would be more serviceable later than white. Lucy found some hand-made cream lace in one of her storage trunks along with the cream-colored veil she had worn at her own first wedding.

Saturday, Ruth and Ida had moved furniture in the McEvans' tiny two-room cabin. Timothy had shared a room with the two boys, while Ruth occupied the other room. A curtain now divided Ruth's old room into two cubicles. An addition to the cabin was planned for later in the summer, but for now

Ruth would share her already minimal space with her brothers. When Ida apologized for the third time for making Ruth give up her room, the teenager stopped tucking in the sheets around Phillip's bed to look straight at her. "I've prayed for a long time that God would let you be our next mother. Why should I complain since He's answered my prayer?" Tears welled in Ida's eyes remembering Ruth's sincerity. How she wished her own mother could share this day with them! Busyness had kept thoughts of Mom in the foggy background of her mind. Now emotion threatened to overwhelm. What would she have thought of Timothy?

A handkerchief dabbing at her cheeks brought her back to reality. "I didn't tell you to start crying and turn your eyes all red!" Lucy's scolding brought a shaky smile to Ida's face. "That's better. What is your bridegroom going to think of you crying on your wedding day?"

Ida recalled his gentle smile on previous occasions when her emotions had overflowed. "He'd just give me his handkerchief. He's used to tears by now." In the three months since he'd proposed, they'd spent every possible moment together, talking while they cleaned the barn, repaired the corral, cooked supper, or just sat in Lucy's parlor. Her love for him grew as he continued to struggle to share his heart. While they worked to make sure the children didn't feel left out, Lucy, Nina, and Cynthia worked equally hard to give them plenty of time for private discussions, as well. Despite their short and strange courtship, Ida felt friendship and love had grown together. They had become as much best friends as sweethearts.

The door rattled. Before Ida could get up for another peek, Ida pushed her firmly back into the chair. "I'll check this time." She moved the curtain slightly, then looked over her shoulder with a broad smile. "He's here now. You can relax."

Ida heard the beloved, familiar tread approaching their cubicle moments before Cynthia's stern, "Don't you dare, Timothy McEvan. She'll be out when it's time."

It seemed to take forever for everyone to get settled, then Lionel started playing on his guitar "All the Way My Saviour Leads Me." Cynthia had offered to have Doug move the piano to Spencers' cabin so she could play a traditional wedding march. Though touched by her offer, Ida and Timothy had agreed the hymn would be most meaningful for their wedding. When their friends started singing, Lucy finally allowed Ida to step out of hiding. Only a half-dozen steps separated her from her groom and the visiting preacher who would unite them. Timothy's beaming smile made the effort to surprise him worth it. She couldn't have stopped her own answering grin if she'd wanted to.

The preacher spoke briefly of the love between man and wife being an earthly symbol of the love between Christ and His church. Timothy and Ida gazed at each other throughout the short sermon, silently giving and accepting commitment. She revelled in the gentle affection in his eyes. For once, no hint of pain hovered there. Each of them had come a long way to find the other. Together they stood as testimony to God's ability to turn heartache into peace.

"Do you, Ida Thomas, take this man to be your wedded husband, to love and comfort him, for richer or for poorer, in sickness and in health, until death do you part?" The preacher's formal question brought an answer straight from her heart.

"I do."

Author's Note

On November 11, 1930, the town of Dawson Creek completed moving its buildings to a new location two and one-half miles northeast to be nearer the approaching railway line. Details of the move are similar to descriptions in this book. Passenger service ended at the town of Hythe until January 15, 1931, when Dawson Creek's first passenger train arrived. All other events and characters in this book are fictitious.

A Letter To Our Readers

Dear Reader:

In order that we might better contribute to your reading enjoyment, we would appreciate your taking a few minutes to respond to the following questions. When completed, please return to the following:

Rebecca Germany, Editor
Heartsong Presents
P.O. Box 719
Uhrichsville, Ohio 44683

1. Did you enjoy reading *River of Peace*?
   ☐ Very much. I would like to see more books
      by this author!
   ☐ Moderately
      I would have enjoyed it more if _____

      _____

2. Are you a member of *Heartsong Presents*? Yes   No
   If no, where did you purchase this book? _____

   _____

3. What influenced your decision to purchase this
   book? (Check those that apply.)

   ☐ Cover   ☐ Back cover copy

   ☐ Title   ☐ Friends

   ☐ Publicity   ☐ Other _____

4. On a scale from 1 (poor) to 10 (superior), please rate the following elements.

    ___Heroine   ___Plot

    ___Hero   ___Inspirational theme

    ___Setting   ___Secondary characters

5. What settings would you like to see covered in *Heartsong Presents* books?

_____

_____

6. What are some inspirational themes you would like to see treated in future books?_____

_____

_____

7. Would you be interested in reading other *Heartsong Presents* titles?   ❑ Yes   ❑ No

8. Please check your age range:
❑ Under 18   ❑ 18-24   ❑ 25-34
❑ 35-45   ❑ 46-55   ❑ Over 55

9. How many hours per week do you read? —————

Name _____

Occupation _____

Address _____

City _____ State _____ Zip _____

···· Hearts ♥ng ····

Any 12 *Heartsong Presents* titles for only $26.95 *

HISTORICAL ROMANCE IS CHEAPER BY THE DOZEN!

Buy any assortment of twelve *Heartsong Presents* titles and save 25% off of the already discounted price of $2.95 each!

plus $1.00 shipping and handling per order and sales tax where applicable.

HEARTSONG PRESENTS TITLES AVAILABLE NOW:

...... Presents ......

Great Inspirational Romance at a Great Price!

Heartsong Presents books are inspirational romances in contemporary and historical settings, designed to give you an enjoyable, spirit-lifting reading experience. You can choose from 100 wonderfully written titles from some of today's best authors like Colleen L. Reece, Brenda Bancroft, Janelle Jamison, and many others.

When ordering quantities less than twelve, above titles are $2.95 each.

Hearts♥ng Presents
Love Stories Are Rated G!

That's for godly, gratifying, and of course, great! If you love a thrilling love story, but don't appreciate the sordidness of popular paperback romances, **Heartsong Presents** is for you. In fact, **Heartsong Presents** is the *only inspirational romance book club*, the only one featuring love stories where Christian faith is the primary ingredient in a marriage relationship.

Sign up today to receive your first set of four, never before published Christian romances. Send no money now; you will receive a bill with the first shipment. You may cancel at any time without obligation, and if you aren't completely satisfied with any selection, you may return the books for an immediate refund!

Imagine. . .four new romances every month—two historical, two contemporary—with men and women like you who long to meet the one God has chosen as the love of their lives. . .all for the low price of $9.97 postpaid.

To join, simply complete the coupon below and mail to the address provided. **Heartsong Presents** romances are rated G for another reason: They'll arrive *Godspeed!*